YA GRI
35245002459147
14ya
Griffin, Adele
Tighter

Greenfield Public Library
5310 West Layton Avenue
Greenfield, WI 53220

MAY 2017

TIGHTER

D0968877

More critically acclaimed novels from Adele Griffin

All You Never Wanted

The Julian Game

Picture the Dead

*Where I Want to Be**

*Sons of Liberty**

*National Book Award finalist

Flip to the back for an excerpt from Adele Griffin's
new novel, *All You Never Wanted*.

TIGHTER

ADELE GRIFFIN

GREENFIELD PUB LIBRARY
5310 W. LAYTON AVENUE
GREENFIELD, WI 5322 0

EMBER

This is a work of fiction. Names, characters, places, and incidents either are the product of the author's imagination or are used fictitiously. Any resemblance to actual persons, living or dead, events, or locales is entirely coincidental.

Text copyright © 2011 by Adele Griffin
Cover photograph copyright © 2012 by Clayton Bastiani/Trevillion Images

All rights reserved. Published in the United States by Ember, an imprint of Random House Children's Books, a division of Random House, Inc., New York. Originally published in hardcover in the United States by Alfred A. Knopf, an imprint of Random House Children's Books, New York, in 2011.

Ember and the E colophon are registered trademarks of Random House, Inc.

Visit us on the Web! randomhouse.com/teens

Educators and librarians, for a variety of teaching tools, visit us at randomhouse.com/teachers

The Library of Congress has cataloged the hardcover edition of this work as follows:
Griffin, Adele.
Tighter / Adele Griffin.
p. cm.
Summary: Based on Henry James's "The Turn of the Screw," tells the story of Jamie Atkinson's summer spent as a nanny in a small Rhode Island beach town, where she begins to fear that the estate may be haunted, especially after she learns of two deaths that occurred there the previous summer.
ISBN 978-0-375-86645-6 (trade) — ISBN 978-0-375-96645-3 (lib. bdg.) — ISBN 978-0-375-89643-9 (ebook)
[1. Death—Fiction. 2. Ghosts—Fiction. 3. Nannies—Fiction. 4. Social classes—Fiction. 5. Emotional problems—Fiction. 6. Mental illness—Fiction. 7. Rhode Island—Fiction.] I. Title.
PZ7.G881325Ti 2011
[Fic]—dc22
2010025301

ISBN 978-0-375-85933-5 (pbk.)

RL: 6.5

Printed in the United States of America
10 9 8 7 6 5 4 3 2 1
First Ember Edition 2012

Random House Children's Books supports the First Amendment and celebrates the right to read.

for Q. , *for* M .

No, no—there are depths, depths! The more
I go over it, the more I see in it, and the more I
see in it, the more I fear. I don't know what I
don't see—what I *don't* fear!

—Narrator, *The Turn of the Screw*
by Henry James

ONE

The last thing I did before I left home was steal pills.

"Wait!" I raised my finger and did the *oops* smile, then sprinted back inside while Mom stayed in the car to take me to the train station. First to Teddy's bathroom to swipe painkillers—we were an athletic family, prone to sports-related injury—and then to my parents' stash. Mom's allergies, Dad's insomnia.

Maybe fifty, all in. A good haul, but would it be enough?

Pills were new for me. I'd been sucked in innocently enough, after a track hurdle that ripped some tissue. A major lower-lumbar strain, the doctor had diagnosed. When the pain persisted, I'd started therapy at the Y, which just became another thing to skip. And pill filching was easier.

Now here it was late June and I wasn't an addict, not at all, but the heat packs and aspirin hadn't been getting it done for weeks.

The pills also helped me not think too hard about Mr. Ryan. Sean. I'd called him Sean, a couple of times, in the end. And I was so tired of thinking about him. I gripped a small fantasy that the moment I set foot on Little Bly, he'd evaporate from my memory.

Mom honked. I wavered in the doorway of my bedroom, so safe and familiar. I shouldn't be leaving home. I was worse than anyone knew—not my parents, not my best friend, Maggie. Maybe I needed more than pills, but I'd already swiped such a haul.

I stepped inside, gravitating toward my bookshelf. What to take? What would help? The book of poems Tess gave me last birthday that I'd skimmed and liked. My old *Mother Goose's Nursery Rhymes*, which I'd read so many times in childhood that the cover was unhinging from its spine.

On impulse, I popped them both into my satchel. Not much, but comforting, a double shield to protect me from homesickness. Then I stood, helplessly searching—what more had I forgotten? Surely there was something else, something better—before the horn jounced me from my trance.

"Everyone falls in love with Little Bly. The beaches, the houses." Mom had been nervous-chatting the whole ride. Now we stood by the tracks, waiting for the train to pull in. "This'll be so relaxing! I wish I could come along. At the very least, Jamie, I bet it will be therapeutic for you."

I nodded and yawned. These past weeks, Mom had been big into telling me what Little Bly would be "at the very least." I'm not sure either of us had a clue what it might be at the very most.

But a yawn or a "you said it" were my best conversation stoppers in this summer of limited energy. Not that anything was stopping Mom.

All I really knew, *at the very least*, was that I'd be farther from Maplewood than I'd ever been, outside of a chorus trip to Vienna three years ago, in eighth grade.

"A nice change for you, Jamie."

I nodded again and flattened my hand against my satchel, where my Ziploc bag was stashed. Nice change or not, it was happening. Mom had moved pretty quickly, too, rearranging my life one night while she and Dad were out at a dinner party. She'd made it seem like luck, but her secret motive—her trial kick out of the nest for her youngest, her hang-around-the-house kid—wasn't lost on me.

And I couldn't discount that this was my dullest summer on record. Maggie was off with her family touring a handful of national parks, all of them gone cold turkey off wireless networks as they hopscotched from Appalachia to Yosemite in their Trail-Manor RV. The twins were gone, too—they'd left right after graduation. Teddy, for college football training in Orlando, while Tess was in Croatia teaching English in a one-room schoolhouse. She sent postcards that told us the weather (broiling hot, every day) and what she was eating (beef on a stick, every day). We stuck the cards on the fridge next to pictures Teddy emailed of himself as a dot in a helmet.

So maybe it was my turn to be a body in motion. Specifically, a blur on the Jersey Transit to Penn Station, then all aboard Amtrak's Northeast Corridor bound for Providence, Rhode Island, where I'd catch another local train and then a ferry to the island of Little Bly. My last major trip this week had been my hour at the Y, and then into town to drop off some movie rentals. I felt unsteady and out of shape, and maybe not totally prepared for the direct thrust of a voyage out.

As the train approached, I could feel myself collapsing. No, no, this was a bad idea. I was scared to be jerked out of my orbit like this; I wasn't steady in my head. But I couldn't find the right words to explain any of it to my mother—especially since she was so hopeful that Little Bly was my cure.

A cheery smile, a confident bound up the train steps. I went for the window seat so I could wave as I watched Mom turn miniature. And then with sweating fingers, I sank back and took a pill from the Baggie, swallowing it dry and tasting its bitter silt in the back of my throat. Okay, okay. One step at a time, and I'd be okay. I settled in, rechecking my books, my notebook, my wallet, then unfolding the printout of Miles McRae's email that I'd slipped into my journal. Even though I'd looked at this note so many times I could have sung it.

Dear Jamie,

Great talking to you on the phone the other day. You must hear it from everyone, how much you sound like your mom. I'm glad you've agreed to stay at Skylark for part of the summer, and want to confirm by note our agreed dates, 28 June–7 Aug.

A few punch points. Little Bly is a small island town (about a thousand year-rounders, but the population septuples in summer season). We've got cars, but half the time folks hoof it or bike—help yourself to mine, in the garage. Most of the land is nature reserves or private tracts, and landowners don't care about friendly trespassing (I don't). Walk any direction and you'll hit the beach. Blyers are a kick-back bunch, and you'll see that people aren't "snobs" once they know who you are.

Connie has an ATM card. Tell her what purchases she needs to make. Please don't use any of your own money on Isa.

On that, I set up an automatic pay transfer every other Friday. It should hit your account same day.

One Last Thing. The time zone in Hong Kong is exactly twelve hours different from Little Bly. If you need me, I'm only a call or text away, but don't alert me to crises that I can't control—example: "Where are the beach passes?" Not only won't I know, but I'm too far to hop a plane and hunt them down. It'll only make me feel like a Bad Dad that I'm not around to micro-engineer. Your mother assures me you've got a good head on your shoulders. I'm relying on that.

This should work out perfectly, right? Still can't believe that I'm writing freckle-nosed Sandy Henstridge's daughter. Everyone tells me you're the spitting image of her. Lucky you.

Regards,

M.M.

In my mind, I pictured Miles McRae as a martini-sipping, tuxedo-wearing "Bond, James Bond" type. Maybe because I knew he was rich, and because Mom's face turned as pink as a peppermint when she mentioned him. Presumably, Miles didn't know I existed until last month, when Mom ran into him at the Wolfingtons' dinner party.

"McRae, Miles McRae" might have been surprised to hear that I'd always known about him. Mom had dated Miles a hundred years ago, but she'd kept tabs, the way women do. The way I might on Sean Ryan though he'd left New Jersey to teach high school chemistry in Telluride. No forwarding email—although I'd chased him down online and found him in the school directory.

But Mom's relationship with Miles had always sounded sweet. Also, his wife had died many years ago, of leukemia, and this had been the sad fact percolating in my mind after Mom had arrived home that night, squeaking with a girlishness that made me feel embarrassed for her.

The widower Miles, "still *so* good-looking," had been seated right across the table from her, and at some point between the salad and the blackberry tart, Mom won me my job.

"He hasn't changed," Mom had assured me, as if I'd have a clue how to tell the difference. "He's in Hong Kong overseeing a hotel project, and he wanted to find an au pair—a young person, not his housekeeper—to look after his daughter. To take her to tennis and the beach. Isn't it perfect? You'd stay at their summer home—they're in Beacon Hill during the school year."

The tiniest note of grandeur had crept into Mom's voice as she exhaled these words: *au pair, summer home, Beacon Hill.*

She'd grown up richer than we were now, in that toity world of *summering*, and the Wolfingtons were friends from her youth— which was why that night Mom had crunched her toes into heels and salon-styled her hair into a first-lady flip.

"You just want me out of the house," I'd complained.

"Of course I do. You've been mopey, Jamie. And now here's a job—a paying one, a fun one—that's dropped right in your lap. At the very least, it's an adventure."

"You said it." While Mom didn't push it right there, I knew the plan was all but tied up in ribbons. *Mopey* was Mom's determinedly cheerful shorthand for the thick-walled depression I'd been trapped behind all spring. A taste of her old life, those carefree days when she'd been freckle-nosed Sandy Henstridge, might be just what the doctor ordered.

Time away. Sea air. No parents. I'd return suntanned and worldly. *Pussy cat pussy cat, where have you been?* Maybe Mom was onto something. Maybe that's how the mopeys got zapped. Of course, my other Atkinson relatives hadn't exactly mastered solutions for moping. My dad's brother Uncle Jim had hanged himself on his twenty-first birthday, and my second cousin Hank Wilcox had put a bullet in his brain three years ago after the bank repossessed his house. And what neither of my parents knew was that Uncle Jim and Hank had started to appear to me, claiming me in secret hours as one of their own. My eyes would open into darkness—not in terror, not yet—to find them right there, in my room. The rope skewed around Uncle Jim's neck and Hank staring blankly, the bullet wound black as a cigarette burn at his temple.

And then I'd wake up for real, in a gasp, my heart beating

fast as rain, my newly identified lumbar muscles—extensor, flexor, oblique—pulsing the nerve roots of my spine.

By then, they'd be gone.

Maybe they wouldn't follow me to Little Bly. It was another hope to hold on to.

The pill and the rock of the train lulled me *old mother goose when she wanted to wander would ride through the air* and I slept.

TWO

Connie was awful.

She was also my first bad news of the day. Until then, I'd been caught up in the Bly mystique—the water slapping the sides of the ferryboat, the brine-y cup of chowder I'd purchased minutes before boarding and sipped while leaning over the rail, the mineral sweep of ocean and breeze full in my face.

Then there was the Kindly Old Salt who'd helped with my bag and told me I reminded him of a young Audrey Hepburn. On impulse, I'd dressed nostalgically, in an outfit that teenage Sandy Henstridge might have worn, white camp shirt and capris and my ballet flats. Better than pretty, the Salt had made me feel legitimate—*bonjour! I summered!*—as I popped my nylon wheelie suitcase along the dock, maneuvering around baby strollers and straw bags and ice coolers.

She saw me first. She was short, with a gray poodle perm and matching gray, wide-set shark eyes. "Linen panth," she said, her voice lisping on her *s*, a speech impediment I instantly disliked. "One way to tell you're not a local." Beneath what she seemed to think passed for a charming opener, I detected an annoyance that she'd had to drive out here and fetch me.

When adults suck, as Connie clearly did, it's been my experience that you've got two choices. You can spend all your time buttering them up, plaster-casting your grin and molding your body language so that it silently exclaims *like me, please—I am harmless*. Or—and I promise, this is the better idea—you detach. Let them be their own drippy selves, and don't try to win them over, because you never will.

I slung my bag into the trunk and allowed Connie the full embrace of my small-talk-free silence as we drove along the harbor and then up the rocky coastline. She herself didn't speak until we turned inland onto a stretch of road bordered by sea grasses long as hula skirts. "Buhth Road'th the main artery of the island," she told me. "Nearly everything runth off it."

Not a question, no need to answer. Though I did wonder about the road's actual name. Both Road? Booth Road?

We stayed silent a few miles.

"Thkylark'th the highetht point on the island," was her next fact. "Everyone knowth it by name." Stated with pride. Connie was probably one of those creepy locals who'd never been on an airplane, or, for that matter, had ever left Little Bly.

But Skylark was astonishing. Mom had mapped it online, and then estimated its property worth based on other prime oceanfront real estate, but I still wasn't prepared for its beauty, its fanciful gables and turrets, its crisp white latticework and trellises of climbing roses. The flat emerald sail of lawn complemented the pressed pearl-gray sheet of ocean behind it. Everything ironed smooth to suit the view.

"Holy crap." The words fell out before I could stop them, and shamed me. I didn't want Connie to think I was some loser townie who'd never seen a mansion. But I hadn't, not one like this, and I actively repressed speaking my next thought—*and this is just their friggin' summer house!*

Connie said nothing, but I sensed she enjoyed my awe. She seemed to be driving extra slow, allowing me time to marinate in Skylark's splendor versus my comparative irrelevance. I braced myself as the tires ground hard against the bleached crushed-shell drive, then strained against gravity as we shifted gears and rumbled up.

I never stopped looking at the house. It reminded me of a ship. A ship that had been tossed clean from the sea by some monster storm to survive intact on the cliff above.

From a third-floor window, I saw the shadow of someone observing us drive in, but once the car stopped, the curtain twitched and the figure moved off. It's never a good feeling, that prickle of being watched. Who was it? I frowned up. Then yawned, fake and on purpose—as if to ensure that whoever was looking down on me didn't think that I cared.

We got out, and I followed Connie up the planked steps that led to a wraparound porch, and through the front door, which looked too big to spring open at the turn of the knob, though this is exactly what happened as Connie made it clear that she was Top Dog by bullying in ahead of me. The foyer—a term with which I was now familiar from Mom's reading off the Little Bly real-estate sites—was big enough that you could park a couple of cars inside it, and was decorated in a harmony of tropical Life Savers colors: banana, melon, fruit punch. Walnut floors buffed to glowing bordered the carpets, and the living and dining rooms were filled with delicate antiques. Painted vases crowded every surface and bloomed with arrangements of starflowers, baby's breath and elephant's ear. One thing was obvious: Connie was nuts for this house. Every room she showed me was immaculate. All it needed was a bride descending the stairs.

Instead, it only had us going up; Connie lisping house rules in the rushed voice of a person who loves to talk more than she gets to, and me stubbornly silent and frankly still grumpy about that linen-pants comment.

Colors deepened as we ascended. At the landing, the stained-glass window of Noah gathering animals into his ark filtered hues of orange, cherry and lemon into a pattern of light over the carpet runner. Down wide corridors hung with family portraits, I noticed the ancestral repeat of teardrop nose and gingery hair. Not beautiful, but dramatic features that carried all the way around to the full-length painting at the end of the hall. Where two redheaded boys and their raven-haired but drop-nosed sister, swathed in dark velvet and white lace, were grouped around a chunky Saint Bernard.

Here, we stopped.

Gawking at the children's sweet faces, I was acutely self-conscious of my blundering intrusion into this cloistered world of genteel innocence. I didn't belong here. I should go while I could.

I hardly noticed the door opposite, until Connie opened it.

14

"You're in the blue room. Which you'll thee ith more than enough." Connie's tone suggested that this wasn't her choice, that I didn't deserve the honor. In her hesitation before she stepped through, I wondered if she hoped I'd do the right thing here and request more suitably humble quarters—preferably nearer to an attic or washing machine.

But I knew from the moment I entered that I wouldn't trade squat. The room was perfect, fit for the princess I would pretend to be. And wasn't that what I needed, most of all? To jump-start myself into the more substantial, confident Jamie Atkinson than the girl who'd whimpered away from the stick in the eye that had apparently qualified as my junior year?

At the very least, as Mom might say, I could play it for laughs. Dig up a tasseled shawl or strip of mink and send pics of myself at the dressing table with a caption like "And how's *your* summer going, dahling?"

"Duth everything thuit you?" Connie asked, all Sylvester the Cat sarcasm, as she opened another door to the en suite bathroom.

I turned from the window in a slow circle, my eyes tracing a line of the room's encompassing beauty, its fireplace and four-poster, its paintings and bookshelves, skirted dressing table and crowned armoire, back to the window with its view of green lawn, blue sky, oyster sea.

"It's the shite." A Maggie-and-me word, a joke word, with a hint of Euro-cool.

But Connie frowned. "Remember your language. A child livth here."

I moved to look out the bathroom window, which had a view

of the pool, an imposing bluestone rectangle so meticulously landscaped that the idea of going for a swim in it seemed disruptive, like a prank. "Where is she, anyway?" I'd been listening for Isa since I'd walked in, but the house was silent. No thumping feet from the upper floor, not a giggle, not even a whisper.

Connie was looking through my bedroom window. I left the bathroom to follow her gaze outward to the lighthouse that stood on a high outcropping of rock, facing Skylark and separated by an inlet. I'd seen it as we'd driven up, but from this angle, the window framed it neat as a painting. "Likely gone out."

I pointed. "As in all the way out there?"

"She yoothed to go out there quite a bit, latht year." The housekeeper turned on me. "The Mithter didn't tell you about what happened here latht year, did he?"

My mind sped through Miles's email. The punch points. The time zone. The request not to bug him. "Is there something I should know?"

Connie didn't answer. She smoothed a pinch in the curtain, stooped to pick a bit of fluff off the carpet, pulled out the handkerchief she kept in her watchband and honked into it. Then retucked the snotty cloth into place. "Go find her, when you're thettled. It wath Jethie who encouraged her to do anything and everything. Though the differenth between a free thpirit and completely thpoiled I mutht be too old to tell." And with an old lady's sigh to prove it, she heaved my suitcase onto a small luggage rack at the foot of the bed and unzipped it, preparing to unpack my things.

I stepped in front of it. "I'll take care of that." Nasty snoop. I'd have to watch out. Find a good hiding place for my Ziploc, for starters. "Who's Jessie, anyway?"

"The girl from latht thummer," said Connie, reluctantly backing off my bag. "The girl who had your job?" Her voice quizzed me.

I shook my head. No, Miles McRae hadn't mentioned Jessie.

Her eyes squinted me in, as if she had special powers to detect me to my core, truthful self. "Jutht ath well. The patht hath no bearing on today." Her lisp made this proclamation sound weirdly ominous. If Maggie had been with me, we'd have laughed.

With no Mags, the moment was unsettling.

I was glad when Connie moved to go. "Our water'th from a cold-thpring well, tho be careful with it; it'th not bottomleth. Try to limit yourthelf to three flutheth per day. With training, it thouldn't be difficult. And it might get chilly early morning, tho cover your feet when you walk on the bare floor. Be back with Itha by theven, for dinner. It'th thpaghetti tonight."

I wanted to ask more about Jessie—like why hadn't she wanted her old job back this summer?—but I'd save my questions for Isa. The less time spent with Connie, the better. So I stood there, unwilling to yield any pleasantries ("Thpaghetti, yum!"). Waiting for her to leave me so that I could unpack, and use up one of my precious toilet flushes.

THREE

After I'd traded my *panth* for jeans, hid my pills behind my books in the bottom bookshelf and texted my parents a quick *hi im here all ok*, I had over an hour to kill before dinner. Connie hadn't pushed too hard for me to find Isa, as long as I got back before the all-important "theven" dinner hour, so I decided not to make it a priority just yet. Besides, I wanted to spend some time adjusting to Skylark.

As I brushed my hair in the mottled mirror over the fireplace, I wished there were more of me to ground the space. I was tall, not thin by any stretch; "strong-boned" was what Dr. Gamba said—which always sounded like a euphemism for something crueler, though nobody could call me fat and be right. But in the rigid grandeur of this room, I felt formless and misplaced. Like I could float to the ceiling and bob around the amber-globe chandelier.

Or maybe it was just the effects of the pill.

Once, Mr. Ryan had said I was beautiful. That I reminded him of a cat. His imagination transformed my round eyes, flattish nose and mini-bite mouth into something playful and feline. He was just out of college, he'd confessed during one of our chicken-nachos afternoons in the way-back booth of Ruby Tuesday. Not only was he hardly earning any salary, but his student loans were killing him. He'd wanted to quit every single day, he said. He felt like he'd sold his soul to the "collective critique of suburban high school entitlement." Except for me, he'd said.

"Again and again, I looked to your gentle face as a beacon."

I had a feeling he'd practiced these poetic phrases before-hand, though Sean Ryan was a chemist at heart, the way he knew how to ignite my imagination and dissolve my willpower . . . no, I wasn't going there.

I was months and miles past all that.

Halfway down the corridor, I doubled back for another pill. Whatever I'd taken on the train, it was waning.

A late-afternoon mist had drifted over the sea, hiding the sun and weighting the air. I'd kicked off my flats, and my feet felt the sting of unfamiliar objects, shards of mussels' shell and nips of rock, as I picked my path to the lighthouse. At first it had seemed like a no-brainer. Down the hill, bisect the inlet; find the uphill path and billy-goat up, up, up.

But the water between the bluffs was rougher than I'd antici-pated, waves smashing in and out of the gullies. Black eelgrass noosed tight around my ankles as my jeans soaked to a water-mark just past my knee, then climbed darkly higher.

At the roar overhead, I looked up to see a private jet wing past, so low and close that while there was plenty of space

19

between us, I instinctively ducked, wetting my upper half to match my lower. The airport must be on this side of the island. It wasn't hard to picture all the fabulous Little Blyers coasting in from the city on their propjets, right on time for lobster thermidor. Capital M Money lived here. I could see it in the peaked roofs along the coast, the lush gardens and hedgerows bordering properties spread out so far that not a decibel of someone else's noise polluted the ears of his neighbor.

I didn't know much about the Very Rich. The most glamorous kid in my class was Dex Benten, whose parents once attended the Academy Awards because they'd composed the sound tracks for the *Bourne Identity* franchise. Dex's house had an eternity pool and he drove a used BMW, but that wasn't much to throw around. That wasn't private planes and homes with names, and for a sea-soaked moment, I felt completely manipulated onto this island. Who was I, some Victorian waif suffering from a Mystery Lung Disease, where the only cure was exile and isolation? This wasn't my scene at all. And I didn't know a soul.

When it had been an abstraction, Little Bly had sounded almost exhilarating. Here, in the tidal, crashing reality, I was struck by how desperately lonely I might be for the next six weeks.

What. The hell. Was I doing here?

Jerking myself from my thoughts, I began to move fast, wading out with long strides into the ocean, but I still couldn't crack how to approach the hard profile of rock surrounded by its moat of sucking shoals. Eventually, I gave up, retracing my steps until I was back on land below Skylark again. The only other way in was to return to the house, then head down the hill on its opposite side and skirt around to the back of the lighthouse. Eating up another twenty minutes, minimum.

I measured it. Even an unsuccessful attempt was better than returning to Connie, who'd no doubt find me some mind-numbing, pre-dinner kitchen tasks. She was just that type.

Anywhere but back. I'd keep going.

And as it turned out, once I'd scaled the hill, I found a wooden walk secured on its ocean side by a rail. I took it and became instantly engrossed with watching my feet; my pedicure was so chipped it showed more toenail than polish. So when I finally did look up, I stopped cold, my heart jumping in surprise.

Either I was going deaf, or the kids hadn't made a sound.

There were two of them, standing a dozen yards ahead where the rail ended, at the edge of a jut of overhang. I shaded my eyes. One painkiller's side effect was occasionally a fuzzy double image, but this was no trick of the eye.

Two same-sized girls in shorts and T-shirts. Or maybe a girl and a skinny, shortish guy?

The longer I looked, the more I was sure, yes, definitely a guy, but not so shrimpy as the girl was tall. And they were shar-ing a private moment. There was a leaning-in-ness and face-to-face-ness about them. They must not have seen me yet, either, and so I started self-consciously clearing my throat—though nei-ther of them reacted. Maybe they were neighbors—part of the "kick-back bunch" of Little Blyers that Miles McRae talked about. If I could make a couple of friends right from day one, then I wouldn't have to

"Jamie!"

At the sound of my name, I snapped around.

She was a flit of white high above, her arms making broad arcs, as if she needed rescuing. Standing in front of the lighthouse, she seemed as matched to it as a Dutch girl guarding her windmill. I signaled back as I swerved off the walk and broke into a jog to meet her, glancing back over my shoulder at the couple.

Only they weren't there, and in my next breath, the late afternoon sun had burned through the haze to shine harsh in my eyes. I spun around, confused—*whoa whoa wait wait*, where had they gone? Had they climbed down, or dived off that rock? No way, it was so high. But I had to know, and I veered in the opposite direction, running to look over the edge of the cliff. I hadn't been too aerobic since my injury, and by the time I reached the place where they'd been, I could feel the burn in my lungs and gently used muscles.

Nothing. Nothing below but the phlegm of foam breaking over the peaks of rock. The tide was coming in. I caught my breath. Had they jumped? For real? The water didn't seem deep enough; any kind of long-drop jump looked incredibly dangerous. Maybe they'd climbed down quick, a pair of romantic sand crabs, and then scuttled off to some secret grotto, but the timing of that was almost impossible.

"Jamie! Over here!"

I turned again to face Isa, who was now gliding down the hill. She was even prettier than the picture Miles had jpged. On our one phone call, he'd told me that Isa had been adopted as an infant from Vietnam ("though she reminds me of my late wife anyway. Something about her laugh, it breaks my heart, go figure"), and her sandalwood skin and gourmet-chocolate eyes looked as if they'd been warmed by sunshine. She radiated with such a näive, delicate sweetness that it was hard not to automatically want to reflect some of it as I smiled back at her.

"Jamie, right? You're such a honey, coming out here to find

me," she said. Calling me a honey seemed like a quirky, almost antiquated thing for an eleven-year-old girl to do. Except Isa wasn't your typical almost–seventh grader. I could tell that at once; she wasn't one of those girls trend-surfing on wash-out henna tattoos, retro T-shirts or the glitter body makeup that I'd forever associate with Maggie's and my junior high experience— a two-year recipe of Trying Too Hard with a major pinch of Not Getting It.

Isa's nearly waist-length hair and eyelet cotton dress were more old-fashioned and whimsical than anything I'd have been caught dead in at that age. But when she briefly took my hand in greeting, the needy pressure of her grip reminded me of the way I'd once grasped Mr. Ryan's fingers under the table at Ruby Tuesday. My squeezing hand, my urgent and devoted stare. I'd been just as much a child, in my own way. And yet it also seemed like a long time ago, too, when I'd felt such innocence.

"What's wrong?" Isa stepped back to scrutinize me. "You looked at me funny."

"I'm sorry." I smiled. In the bright sun it felt like I was grimacing. "Nice to meet you."

She squinted at me, then grinned. "Me too. It's been maximum boring here, especially since Milo's away at camp this summer, which leaves just me and the Funsicle, who hates to drive me places or do anything cool. The Funsicle even hates music. Once I asked her what kind, and she said the musical kind."

"Who's the Funsicle?"

"Connie. It's her nickname. Jessie made it up because she said Connie's the Grim Reaper of Fun. As in, if she thinks people are having a good time, she slices it to the ground."

"I like that. Fun sickle. And who's Milo?"

"My older brother."

"I don't think your dad mentioned him."

"Probably since you'll never meet him. You're just for me, after all. Milo's away till August. Which is too bad. Miley's the man. He's major gorgie—all my friends say. And he's sweet when he's not intense. Sucks he's fourteen or you'd have fallen madly in love with him."

"Maybe it's better that he's not around to distract me."

I'd been kidding, but Isa seemed to take my comment sincerely. "That's true."

"Hey, Isa"—I said her name tentatively; she was the first Isa I'd ever known—"did you see those kids up there?"

"What kids? I've been alone all day, losing my mind from boredom. When I saw you drive up, I was, like, Fine-Ally." She spun out in a twirl of black hair and white dress. "My dad told me he went out with your mom way back."

"Over thirty years ago," I said. "It's weird to imagine those days—before the Internet, right?"

"It's weirder to imagine my dad young," she said, giving me a look like perhaps she'd overestimated me. "C'mon. Let's go down. I made mint lemonade." As she yanked me toward the walk, her shackle on my wrist was too intense for me to run more than a quick check over my shoulder, to where the kids had stood.

I had seen them, hadn't I? I knew I had.

"Connie hates anyone to be late," Isa warned as we approached the house. "'Theven meanth theven.' Jess always used to say Connie'd chop off three of your fingers if you'd let her, to remind you what time to be home for dinner."

24

I snorted. I liked that. "So where is your Jessie this summer?"

Isa regarded me. Her face was a golden, heart-shaped locket, with every feature scrolled into place like a careful calligraphy. Pretty as she was now, in a few years she'd be a knockout. I was also struck, even before she spoke again, by the sadness in her face now that her smile was gone.

"Jessie's dead," she answered.

FOUR

We arrived at the house to find a van stenciled with the sign LIT-
TLE BLY LIVERY 1-800-BLY-RIDE parked outside the wide-open
front door, where Connie emerged clutching a fistful of bills.

"Dad's home?" I heard the catch of hope in Isa's voice. "Yes
way! To surprise us!" She looked at me gleefully, but my mind
was still reeling with the new information.

Jessie, this my-age girl who'd held my job, this fun-loving,
Connie-defying girl with whom I'd felt an instant bond based on
those few facts, was *dead*.

How? Why? When? Had she lived at Skylark? What happened to her?

Isa hadn't wanted to go into details, so I'd played it casually.
Letting her ramble about the lemonade she'd made for me—
using mint she'd picked herself from the kitchen garden—and

recount her past performance this spring when she and her friend Clementine had put on a play based on the Robert Frost poem "Mending Wall" for their entire sixth-grade class.

At my school, you'd get your butt kicked for inflicting anything that tedious on your fellow students. But I could already see that Isa was a more fragile specimen than Mags and me at the height of our wedgie-yanking, middle school powers.

"Here." Connie was hopping down the steps to shove the money through the passenger-side window at the cab driver. "It'th not much but it'th not my fault, either, hadn't got a chanth to get into town to . . ." Whatever she said next was obscured by wheels spinning as the driver took his lame tip and roared off.

Whoever had arrived, I wouldn't be making a killer impression. Not in my wet clothes and sweaty face. Isa herself was adjusting one of her dress straps and shaking back her hair.

"Is it Dad? It's Dad, right?"

"No," said Connie, "it'th Dr. Hugh. And he'th only thtaying for dinner, and don't bother him for caramel."

"Dr. Hugh, cool." Though Isa still looked disappointed as she darted into the house. "Dr. Hyoooooo! Did you bring me any caramels?"

"Her thychiatritht," explained Connie. "He popped over to check in. Hardly enough dinner for everyone, but there'th nothing I can do."

I followed her into the house and to the kitchen, where a man who looked like one of the Smith Brothers cough-drops guys— the one with the *Guitar Hero* beard—stood formally in his summer suit accepting the glass of lemonade Isa had poured him.

But as soon as I entered, the doctor's eyes snapped like a

terrier bite to my face. And I knew he'd come not just to check on Isa, but also to see about me.

"Hello! You're the babysitter? Jamie Atkinson?"

I nodded. "'Scuse me. Just going to wash up." I pivoted and ran for it. Up the stairs, down the three turns of hallway to my bedroom, where I locked my bathroom door and stayed there a few minutes, working on some calming breaths.

I hated doctors, I really did. I wasn't even too crazy about Dr. Gamba, and she'd been the family doctor since forever. But the whole medical profession freaked me out the way they always wanted more from you. More answers about your health, more information about your weight and your eating habits and when was the last time you fill-in-the-embarrassing-blanked.

A quick splash of water on my face and a few drags of my brush through my hair ate up another minute or so.

"Relax," I told my reflection. "This guy is just some country-fried shrink. He's not out to dissect you." But then I dawdled, rearranging the pink soap pigs on their dish. Why had Isa been seeing a psychiatrist? What was wrong with her? Did it have anything to do with what had happened last summer?

McRae certainly had been sparse with the details of this job. Talk about being thrown in the deep end. And I didn't even have Mags. I didn't have anyone.

Okay, deal. Game face. One final, unnecessary flush of the toilet—*take that, Funsicle*—and I left.

Motoring out the door to the corridor, I smashed right into him.

"Oh! Sorry." I jumped back. "Sorry, sorry," I repeated.

Behind us, the three portrait children stared.

Maybe it was the slightly affected way he stood there, a bit defiant, a bit entitled, like a rock star at his microphone. Or maybe it was that he so sharply echoed my imaginings of his rogue charmer father. But I knew straight off that this was Milo McRae.

"No, my bad," he said, uncaring. "Who're you?"

"Jamie. The babysitter. Or au pair, whatever."

"Hi-larious. You gonna spoon-feed me applesauce and put me in my pj's?"

"I'm here for Isa."

"Yeah, I know." He appeared more relaxed than I was. "I'm the prodigal Milo."

I didn't answer. We took each other in. Most fourteen-year-old boys were a pathetic misery of blackheads and hormones. Not this one. Isa hadn't exaggerated. He was handsome. More than handsome. I could see in a minute that this was the kid who bought the beer, the kid who broke the locks and knew the passwords, the kid who'd fooled around with older girls late night in the lodge during his last ski holiday. In some ways, he was also the kid I feared most—the ultimate prepster, with his braided rope bracelet and threadworn boaters that probably matched his S.S. *Trustpuppy* starter sailboat moored over at the Little Bly Yacht Club harbor.

I tried not to stare. I kept staring. Milo looked like he'd just graduated from skinny to slim. Long and lithe, with wavy chestnut hair, olive-dark eyes (the opposite of Sean Ryan—an inevitable comparison—who was vanilla-pink and soft as sponge cake) and a face that would be handsomer, I bet, when he wasn't scowling. Judging me.

He's sweet when he's not intense. Yet Milo seemed like nothing *but* intensity. I could tell even by the way he fell too close in step as I headed for the landing. This kid was a challenge.

"So, you got a visitor's pass from camp? Does Connie know you're here?" I asked.

"Answer one, no, not visiting. Staying. Answer two, yes, she knows. If you'd looked closer, you'd have seen the panic in her eyes."

"How'd you get here?"

"I hitched a ride in from the train station with the doc." At the burst of Dr. Hugh's laughter from below, Milo stopped. I stopped with him. "Hugh and Connie. Might spoil my appetite. Maybe I'll come down later for leftovers."

"Sorry, I still don't get it. Why are you here at all?"

I had a feeling that I wasn't the first girl Milo gifted with that sudden, Cheshire smile. "I got tossed."

"Aha." Thrown out of summer camp. Ideas rockslid through my head—sex, drugs, theft, alcohol? I'd known Milo a minute, and all of it seemed possible.

"Come down to say hi to Isa," I said. "She'd love it."

Milo rolled his eyes but then he pounced past me, down the stairs, off balance as he hit the bottom tread and jumped to reach up, his hand batting the finial of the lantern-style brass light fixture that hung from a linked chain. The light went swinging as Milo skid-landed on the carpet, rumpling it from its matting, and nearly toppling the umbrella holder in the corner.

"He shoots, he scores!" Milo cheered himself. Then turned to see if I was watching.

"Two points," I said.

"Points for who?" Isa had crept up to peep around from the dining room. "Who are you talking to? What's going on?"

"Surprise," I said, pointing. "Milo heard you missed him."

I'd really shocked her. For a moment she stood frozen, dumb-founded, her eyes wide and her shoulders tensed. "Milo?" she whispered. Then she started laughing, amazed, as she crept a few steps closer. "Miley! Miley! You came home! For how long?"

"Till I go." He reached out and palmed her head like a basketball. I could tell Isa wanted more, a hug maybe, but felt shy about it.

"When's that?" she asked.

"Isa, roll with it," he said.

"Okay," she conceded quietly. And I was relieved that while Isa was clearly stunned by the fact of him, she also seemed just as happy with her brother's arrival as with the promise that her dad might have come back. "C'mon, then. Let's eat, Miley."

I followed them both through the dining room, into a sur-prisingly modern but unsurprisingly spotless kitchen. Its corner booth was set with silk napkins, and the silverware was huge, like what rich Vikings might have used. Connie and Dr. Hugh were chatting about local island news, but Milo didn't wait. He ladled up from the pasta bowl.

So I went for the loaf of bread, sawing off a chunk as Isa picked the sesame seeds from the salad.

"Who would win in a fight?" she asked. "An owl or a rac-coon?"

"No thilly talk at dinner," said Connie.

"Owl," I said.

"Raccoon by a landslide," added Milo.

Isa giggled.

"*Adultth* will eat later." Connie gave me a look. I didn't care. Silly talk was the only kind of talk I wanted. Au pair trumps

31

housekeeper on that one. "Jethie, you'll need to look after your and Itha'th kitchen meth."

Milo snorted. "Hear that, Jeth? Gotta handle your own kitchen meth."

"My name isn't Jessie, it's *Jamie*," I corrected loudly.

Connie ignored me, bustling around the pantry to find a bottle of wine for the doctor. I wished he'd just go—he exuded "pompous know-it-all" like a bad odor. After Milo had shot downstairs to the basement-level family room for TV, I challenged Isa to a yodeling contest. Just to annoy the *adultth*.

But I could feel it coming. Hugh looked too purposeful, and when Isa escaped downstairs to join Milo, he followed me through the kitchen door and out to the porch, where I'd been planning to sneak a smoke. Tobacco wasn't one of my addictions, or even habits, but I'd bought a pack of mentholated lites right before I left home, and had stuck one in my jeans pocket while I was upstairs. Just in case I was in the mood for a vice.

"Jamie?"

"You said it."

"Well, no, I haven't, yet. But I did want to note that you've got yourself a set of challenges this summer." Hugh cleared his throat. "As you can see, Isa's a special, sensitive girl." He spoke gravely, as if confiding CIA secrets. He probably read the grocery list the same way. It made me twitchy. "She's always been introverted. More so since the unfortunate—tragic—events of last year."

"You're talking about the other babysitter?"

"Yes."

When I didn't say anything, he continued. "Jessie Feathering died in an accident. It was a terrible thing. Heartbreaking, a shock to the community." Ha, he was practically begging for me to ask for more. No way. I didn't want to get into it, to give Hugh an opportunity to ensnare me in any conversation. Intriguing as this topic was, I could learn the whole deal of what happened to Jessie Feathering from anyone.

In fact, I liked not playing along, not asking the natural questions. It bothered him, I could tell in his eyes.

"I get along great with kids," I said instead. "And Isa's sweet. So, it's all good."

"Yes, well. I very much hope so."

Then I waited for him to go. He didn't. "So, to explain a bit about the island," he started, as if he were answering my question anyway, and then, just like that, he marched off straight into the lecture I'd been hoping to sidestep by not asking about Jessie. Mags had a word for this type of person—a MEGO, as in My Eyes Glaze Over. And Hugh was a total MEGO, right up there with Mags's gramps and my dentist, Dr. Ogilvy.

Now I stood in faint despair as he went on and on and on. "Little Bly, you'll find, is an idyll for the loner . . . and there's plenty to do . . . Isa needs structure and play . . . friends her age and the like."

"Yep, her dad already told me all this." Untrue, but I'd have figured out Isa and Little Bly on my own, eventually. Still he kept going. My eyes were more glazed than a box of Dunkin' Donuts. Why wouldn't he leave me alone already? Finally, perhaps daunted by my unrelenting silence, Hugh decided to wrap it up.

"At any rate, her father asked me to pay this visit. We've been friends since boyhood."

"Then it'll be easy for you to narc on me, if I'm not doing my job right."

That did it. Even the bristles of Hugh's beard seemed to stiffen. "Why, Jamie, it's not my intention to make you feel mistrustful," he said. "I simply want to underline—please don't encourage Isa's wilder bursts of imagination. It's hard for her to distinguish reality from her flights of fancy. Be my scout. If anything troubles you, I've left my phone and email with Connie."

"No problem." I nodded. *Go scout yourself, Doc.* "Thanks for that. Night."

The twins always joked about my problem with authority. Maybe it was because I was the youngest. Maybe it was because I was me. But it wasn't my job to be Hugh's anything. So he could forget that.

The cicadas were loud out here, and the air was delicious, carried in on the hush of wind through long grass. Alone, I tucked deep into a wicker chair, listening to it snap and crunch as it adjusted to my body.

"Ever get the feeling you're being watched?"

I startled. Milo must have crept outside through another door to come around from the other side of the porch. He was smoking a cigarette, and my nostrils flared with desire to light up my own, though now it didn't seem appropriate. I was relieved when he didn't offer me one, but instead strolled to the railing and swung up. Elevated and looking down on me, he seemed to be enjoying himself, and I was sure he was flexing his thigh muscles for my benefit.

"As a matter of fact, yes," I said after a moment. "It's spooky here. Boo! Everyone's watching. The madwoman in the lighthouse is crying for her husband's ship to come in. Out in the ocean, we've got the mermaid who wanted to be a human. Anyone else?"

"Uh-huh," Milo answered, a smile playing at the edges of his lips. "You'll see."

"Are you warning me?"

His smile faded. "I guess I am."

I didn't like the look on his face. I changed subjects. "So why'd they kick you out, camper boy?" I asked. "What'd you do? Hijack a canoe? Cheat in the potato-sack race?"

"Let's just say . . . when I'm bad, I'm bad. I was never gonna stick. Dad won't be surprised when he finds out. He's just like me."

Any reaction other than blasé would put me at a disadvantage, so I dismissed Milo with a flick of my hand. "You're like him, you mean. He came first. And if you're such a rebel, answer me this—could you jump off those rocks at the halfway point up to the lighthouse?"

He frowned. "If I wanted to spend the summer in a full-body cast."

"So, no way, nohow?"

"Eh. You'd have to know the water inside out. It's got different depths, depending on the tide. I mean, *I'd* never do it. So you can cross it off your au pair worry list."

"Kiddo, I'm not babysitting you, just your sister. Go jump off a cliff all day long, as far as I'm liable." Then, to soften it, "What I really mean is, I'm not here to tell you what to do."

He smiled. "Cool. We're gonna get along just fine." Then, out of nowhere, "Do you believe in your soul mate?"

"Sticky question. Define soul mate."

"A person you feel like you knew in another life. You ever make that kind of connection to someone else?"

Annoyingly, all I could picture was Sean Ryan. How for three giddy months, I hadn't cared about myself except as I existed

35

through his eyes. Like if my hair was shiny enough or if my fingernails were buffed clean or if I smelled irresistible whenever he leaned over my shoulder to look at my ChemDraw printouts.

Milo was motionless, watching me. Did he know my secret? A secret that I hadn't even told Maggie? Could he tell I was the type of girl who'd be dumb enough to get semi-seduced (and then fully rejected) by her barely-out-of-school-himself science teacher?

What I didn't want was for Milo to think I was a goopy girl on a quest for summer love.

"Who cares if I have a soul mate? This is my summer to disconnect," I said.

"I care," he said. "I think someone's out there. For each of us."

He sounded so much like Maggie, it was actually comforting. I looked him in the eye and said to him what I would have said to her. "How adorable. Do you also believe in Santa Claus? Or is it just looking at stars that makes you want to talk in clichés?"

He blinked. I'd hurt him. Then he laughed. "Screw you, Jersey Girl."

One thing I hate is when people take a free jab at New Jersey. As if it's the last word in tacky wasteland. I especially disliked it coming from this self-entitled rich kid. Leading me on with his silly poetic thoughts, then reverting to some easy joke about New Jersey when I didn't act all enraptured. Maybe I *would* find my soul mate this summer, on this island. It wasn't the craziest idea. But if I did, I wouldn't be gunning to go tell Milo McRae all about it.

Meantime, I did my best to act unbothered. Leaning back and stretching my arms over my head. "Put out your cancer stick," I told him. "Forcing me to breathe in your secondhand is illegal. Even in New Jersey."

FIVE

They arrived in spite of the deadening effects of my sleeping pill. I'd hoped they wouldn't follow me to Little Bly. I'd even considered not taking anything. But then I popped it on the decent chance it was a muscle relaxer. My grab-bag game always held an element of risk, and the only pill I didn't want was one of Mom's weaker antihistamines. Okay by day, but too thin a blanket for night.

Earlier, I'd knelt by the bookcase and rolled the pill in my fingers. I was tired. Did I really need a send-off? Shouldn't the act of falling asleep be somewhat effortless?

As a compromise, I bit it in half. Sleeping pill. Fifteen minutes later, I was out.

They'd been waiting. Hank was facing me on the small chair by the vanity. Uncle Jim was closer, cross-legged on the duvet I'd pushed to the foot of the bed. The steady pressure of his kneecap against my foot had caused me to wake up, although I'd tried, in my twilit state, to ignore him.

Go *away*.

My vision adjusted. Hank was slumped in his seat the way I imagine he used to watch television: his arms hanging over the sides and his chin doubled, his gaze lifted. They were distant as twin moons, my dependable companions, visible and yet far out of reach as always.

"You don't have to watch over me," I whispered, sitting up. "I think I'll be okay here. Mom was right. I needed the change."

Silence. That's always how it was with Hank and Uncle Jim. They didn't acknowledge our communion. Then I could stare at them all I wanted. That night, like every other night, Uncle Jim wore his too-big navy suit. The rope marks were like tar streaks beneath his collar.

The way everyone remembered it, Uncle Jim had been cheerful that night, downing a glass of birthday champagne and then excusing himself to slip into Granddad's study. A private room with a sturdy ceiling light. He'd done it perfectly, a hangman's noose with coils proportioned exactly to rope thickness, slung in correct position behind his ears. No extra, flopping minutes. He'd been studying to be an accountant, and his death seemed accountably tidy.

The note in his breast pocket had read: *please forgive me*.

Hank's had been the more "predictable" death. Everyone said he'd been "a little off" since boyhood, with a decidedly bad temper. More than once I'd heard family members confess relief that he'd turned that rage on his own body. No note—but my dad's line on that was that Hank often took himself by surprise.

38

I'd been born three years after Uncle Jim died, and I'd only met Hank once, at a long-ago holiday party. Yet they'd both known exactly what it was like for me that night, when I'd stood outside Mr. Ryan's door, unable to breathe, buried alive in the avalanche of the moment.

"Who is it?" the woman had called. I'd gotten a glimpse of a brunette in a twinset.

"Some kid needs directions." Mr. Ryan was already turning away from me.

The shut of the door, the slide of the bolt. I'd stumbled to my car. In motion, my humiliation turned liquid; my eyes were swimming in it and my brain was toxic with it until I got home and dropped a couple of muscle relaxants—one more than I'd been prescribed. I went to bed and let the bath of anesthesia wash over me. Lying numb and motionless, I let my mind slip into the quietest room of myself, and I thought absently of bridges and pills, of filling the tub and drowsing into the courage to slice.

I hadn't. I hadn't sunk my blade or looked beneath the kitchen sink. Instead, I'd fallen asleep. But late that night, Uncle Jim and Hank had come to me for the first time. They couldn't reason with me. They didn't even want to. But they didn't want me to be completely alone, either, if I decided to do it for real. They were family, after all.

That's why they were here now.

"Go away," I whispered. "I hardly thought about anything today. It was only a three-pill day, besides. I'm good." At least until the pills ran out.

this is no place for help for you this is no place for you

Their thoughts kept ghosting my brain waves, over and over, like a skipping needle on a dusty record.

this is no place for help for you this is no place for you

"Jamie!"

Now my eyes opened for real.

"Jamie!" Her breath was hot on my face. "Sorry to wake you up, but I had a really bad dream!"

"Isa. . . ." Groggy, I propped myself on an elbow. "What do you want?"

"I want to get in." So I flipped back the sheet, and she crawled into bed beside me. She smelled like apple shampoo. "I'm still scared." Her eyes fretted through the dark to meet mine. "Is it safe here?"

"Of course it's safe." Though I sensed it, too, a smell of burning and then a flicker in my vision that made me bolt up, spine locked and loaded with fresh pain.

"What?" whispered Isa. "What do you see?"

Nothing. "Nothing. Go to sleep."

Except that someone had been here. Not Uncle Jim, not Hank. Someone else. Watching me from the far corner, by the bookshelf. My pounding heart was sure of it, someone who had left as quickly as he'd entered *Jack be nimble Jack be quick Jack jump over the candlestick* and I thought I detected a whiff of tobacco smoke, faint and fading to nothing, as I pressed the heels of my hands into my eye sockets and then snapped on the lamp, squinting into its bright surge.

No. Whatever, whoever, if anything had been here, it was gone now.

Isa was already asleep again. She hadn't even reacted when the light had switched on.

I snapped it off. Isa's breath was a gentle rise and fall, but as I

40

dropped back on my pillow, her fingers crawled and hooked me at the shoulder as she bumped her forehead against mine, murmuring words too quiet for me to hear.

Then her arm fell like a branch across my neck. Uncomfortable, but I let it be, rather than risk disturbing her.

SIX

I woke late the next morning. Isa was gone. My head felt thick, my body reluctant. I rolled from bed and forced myself to draw the curtains.

In the morning sun, the mark was harshly visible on the carpet.

A cold shiver passed over me. Here it was—my evidence. On instinct, I quickly backed away, my eyes never leaving the mark as I first observed it from a distance, and then approached carefully, as if it might bite. I rubbed at it with my big toe. Then knelt and touched a finger to it. Sniffed.

It looked and smelled like a cigarette burn. But whose? Was it Milo, spying on me and leaving proof? Or maybe there was someone else who lived here, like a boarder? Except that Connie hadn't mentioned anyone like that, and she tended to get very MEGO and persnickety when discussing the details of the house.

Maybe there was a boarder she didn't want me to know about.

Only one thing to do. Today, I'd take a tour. Top to bottom. I'd uncover the hidden staircases and revolving bookshelves, the cloak-and-dagger nooks and crannies. I should have done that yesterday. It would be my first project after breakfast.

Isa had other plans. "Morning, sleepyhead!" She waved a piece of toast. "Connie says you can take me to the beach." She was ready to go, too, in a bikini printed with cherries, along with a scarf that pinned her hair back from her face.

"How about later, when it cools down? The sun looks fierce."

"Except everyone's there *now*." Isa frowned. "It's only six miles. Connie says we can use her car."

"Um . . ." As the au pair, did I have to do whatever Isa wanted? Mom had sworn that au pairing was a way for teenagers to make money while doing things they'd have done anyway. But I didn't want to go to the beach. On the other hand, Isa looked so hopeful that it was hard to disappoint her.

Connie, busy at the kitchen sink, nodded to the fruit smoothie she'd prepared for me, and then returned to sudsing the blender.

"Thanks." I chugged it as Isa pleaded and persisted.

"Please, Jamie? Hey, and I bet Milo'll come with us," she said, loping after me up the stairs and back to my room. My heart was playing scales, wondering if the mark would still be there, or if by some wild possibility it had been a trick of the eye. "Pul-eeze? We're members of Green Hill Beach Club, so we've got a cabana for changing and storage. We can go to the Mud Hut for lunch. And there's a big pool plus a kiddie pool, but last summer someone pooped in the kiddie one, so I never—"

"Look. Look there."

Isa followed my pointing finger to the mark. "Ooh, Jamie,

you might get in trouble for that. Smoking *and* wrecking our nice rug." She paused. Then added, softly, "That's just like *him*. Something he would do."

"Just like who?"

"Jessie's old boyfriend." She went right to the mark and tamped at it in the same way that I had, with her big toe. "But that burn looks fresh, so it's your fault."

"It wasn't me. And Milo smokes, too," I reminded her.

"No," she answered. "He does not."

"Yes, he does."

"You can't just go and blame your mistakes on poor Milo."

I didn't want to get into it with her. "Who else lives at Skylark?"

"Only us four now," said Isa. "The blue room's our best. Most everyone's put in the yellow room down the hall. But Dad told Connie to put you here. He wanted you closer to me."

"What about Jessie? Was she in the yellow room?"

"No, Jessie lived with her mom and dad. Only this summer, Mr. and Mrs. Feathering shut up Crescent House and went to Italy. Can we go to the beach now?"

"Give me ten minutes." I snatched my bathing suit and shorts from the drawer and went to the bathroom to shower and change, then encore-shaved my legs and bikini line at the sink. I didn't want to show up at Green Hill Beach Club looking like some hairy yokel.

Carefully, I tracked the razor up and down, keeping focus, as my mind shuffled the possibilities. Who would possibly want to spy on me? Could Dr. Hugh have sent someone, or maybe he and Connie had decided to—

"Ooooooooh!" Isa's squeal interrupted my thoughts. I dropped the razor and dashed out to find her hopping up and down at my window. "Dad's Porsche is parked out front. I wonder who did that?" She smirked at me. "I think it happened earlier, when you were drinking your smoothie and I went to the bathroom. Which means yay, right? Which means we're going to the beach, right?"

I looked. The lollipop-red sports car was adorable. And Milo, hunkered like a vintage James Dean poster behind the wheel, looked like he was meant for it.

"Your brother doesn't have his driver's license," I said. "What's he doing? Would he really take out the car?"

Isa shot me a wondering look. "No! He wouldn't dare." Then she yanked up the window glass. "Hey, hotshot!"

"Hey, yourself," Milo called up. "I was hoping you potatoes would roll."

I was down the stairs and out the front door in a snap. "What do you think you're doing?"

"Before you issue a warrant, all I wanted was to test-drive her down Bush Road." Milo raised his hands in defense. "Unless you'll do the honor?"

"Just get out."

He swung out leisurely and then leaned against the door, as cocky as a car salesman.

"Yes!" squeaked Isa, joining up. "Let's go!"

"I'm sure your dad doesn't want me to drive this. It probably costs a million dollars just to change the oil."

"He let Jessie drive it," said Isa. Which was exactly what I'd hoped she'd say.

Connie was standing in the door. "If you're gonna go to the

trouble of taking the Porth outta the garage without permithion, the leatht you can do ith drive Itha to the beach," she said. "I wouldn't mind thome peath." And when she went back inside, her slam made its own point.

Isa was already strapping herself into a tiny bucket backseat. Milo sauntered around to the front passenger side and opened the door. "Go west, baby!"

Such a gorgeous machine. It wasn't that I didn't want to drive it. The key slid into the ignition like a Cinderella slipper. *Ah, what the hell.*

As Skylark receded from my rear view, I kept grip on the wheel. Hunched so close I could have licked it. Milo found an indie radio station that I'd have picked myself, and then it was hard not to accelerate as the ocean breeze livened my senses.

"Connie didn't even yell at your brother for sneaking out the car," I shouted to Isa, with a sidelong glance at Milo, who was tipped back in the sun, all haughty profile and closed eyes. "What's his secret?" Connie hadn't challenged Milo on anything, come to think of it. Not on getting kicked out of camp. Or on his bad table manners, or making fun of her lisp. Nothing.

"My secret," said Milo, "is I'm a badass."

"Milo's secret," added Isa, "is that Connie's scared of him."

"Because I'm a badass," said Milo, brushing his hand across my knee as he adjusted the volume.

"Shoo." I swatted him off. And while I didn't believe that Connie was scared of Milo, I could see that she kept a wary distance from non-housekeeperly issues. She made the meals, cleaned up, arranged flowers, tended her kitchen garden and stayed in her tidy world. And that was fine by me.

46

Soon we were flying. The speedometer trembled to forty, fifty, sixty. I turned up the volume. "I love this song."

"Who doesn't?" But I knew Milo was impressed I'd kicked it up a notch, and the conflict twisted in me. *Don't be a show-off, Jamie.* Whatever. No doubt everyone showed off for Milo. He was that kind of kid. It didn't mean anything. *So if it means nothing, then stop.*

"Jessie drove crazy fast, too." Isa's hair was whipping like long black ribbons in the wind. "She was fun just like you."

Instantly I let the speedometer fall and set my hands at three and nine. "Sit back, Isa," I reprimanded.

Green Hill Beach Club looked the way it sounded, whitewashed and trying too hard to be unpretentious. An American flag plus a yellow and blue G.H.B.C. one flapped in kinship from a single flagpole. Past the gates, the club was overstaffed with tanned kids breezing through their summer jobs. Slack-jawed parking valet, cell-phone-texting card swiper, iPod-bopping cabana attendant.

A kick-back bunch, Miles McRae had attested. I didn't see it.

They weren't *un*friendly, but something was off. It wasn't just me. I got a lingering glance from the iPod kid. As we passed the pools, a straw-hatted woman leaned up from her chaise and whispered to her friend. Who flapjacked over and watched us. Next was the goggle-eyed fry cook at the Mud Hut.

"Why are people checking us out like we might be visiting space aliens?" I whispered as we took off down the boardwalk that hugged the dunes to an oceanfront dotted with beach umbrellas in club colors of yellow and blue.

Milo pulled his baseball cap lower over his face.

"Jessie," answered Isa.

"Jessie, your babysitter who died in a car crash Jessie?"

"Plane crash," she corrected. "It hasn't even been a year. It's still on people's minds, I guess. It happened right off the coast. They showed the wreckage on CNN. Peter died, too. Seemed like the whole island went to the funerals." She took a breath.

"Peter was her boyfriend?"

Isa nodded. "I hate talking about it. I miss them. Are you sad, Miley? Is it lame to hold hands?" When he didn't answer, she stuck up her chin, and I could tell he'd wounded her. "Fine, be that way. Mr. Badass."

So I let my own hand drop and rest a moment on the back of Isa's neck, as much to get my own bearings as to offer her comfort. Two deaths, not one. The fact of it overwhelmed me. Would I have come here if I'd known it beforehand? At least I should've had a choice in the matter. Miles McRae might have warned me—at least in a footnote or a P.S. No matter how checked out McRae might be from his kids' lives—according to Connie, the guy wasn't even planning to come back from Hong Kong until Labor Day—he owed telling me.

Finding out this way was not normal. I couldn't help but think it was a deliberately kept secret.

We reached the beach. The crash of the surf made an unfriendly sound, and the horizon looked hard and dark as stone. Milo staked the spot for me to plant and grind the club umbrella as Isa snapped flat three beach towels. "Sunblock me?" she asked. "I've got fifty proof in my bag. Then Milo."

"Just you," I said. "You can do Milo's sunblock yourself." And I spread it like primer paint over her shoulders and back.

Milo took the farthest towel and made a show of flexing, sending a toned ripple across his shoulders. Posing for me, before he launched onto his stomach. He was flirting on purpose. Milo was a devil, a tease. He wanted to see if I'd bite. Probably testing to see if he could bring back some hot story to his posh Boston prep school.

After a few minutes, Isa turned to me with a smile. "Milo's stomach growled. He just whispered that Connie's smoothies taste like crap."

"Oh yeah? Well, I don't appreciate swear words," I said loud and primly, giving it my best au pair.

In response, Milo hawed. Eventually, he stood and jogged down to the surf for a swim. I was pretty sure he was keeping it high and tight for my benefit.

Isa watched him, too. Then she took a couple of tabloid magazines from the beach bag. "My addiction," she said.

I fished out my poetry book.

"*Sailing Alone Around the Room,*" Isa read off the jacket. "What's that about?"

"It's poetry. My addiction," I answered, and I picked a place in the middle, hoping the spine didn't look too obviously uncracked.

"Jessie liked junk," she explained. "Poems are for school, she said. Like Robert Frost."

"So untrue, and you're totally missing out."

"You sound like my friend Clementine. She's kind of nerder-rific."

"All the best people are."

Isa smirked. "Jessie didn't think so. She said it only took a nanosecond to tell dorks from cool kids. And if you were a dork, Jess let you know straightaway."

"Fine, that's wonderful, but I'm not Jessie."

That stopped her. She sank into her junk mag, and I tried reading a few poems. Though I soon realized they were a bit tastier than poems; more like odd, true, human things I liked to imagine Sean Ryan saying in his most brilliant, A-game mood.

But I could feel Isa's eyes on me. Soon she'd tossed aside her magazine. "I might need veneers," she said.

"You do not. Your teeth are perfect. And you're too smart to get sucked in by those awful rags."

Isa waved me off. "Jessie got me hooked. She'd bring them from her house. Now they make me feel close to her."

"No offence to Jessie, but they're still junk. I'll lend you my book if you promise no more tabloids."

"Are you sure?"

"I've read it like a hundred times."

She took it. "Thanks, Jamie. This looks better."

It was such a small thing, but I could tell she was grateful. Maybe I really did have a purpose being here. Maybe my nerder-rific self would be a benefit to Isa, who seemed so lost: old-fashioned and overly mannered one minute, then spinning off in whatever direction you placed her in the next. It was as if she only existed as a manifestation of what other people wanted her to be. It sounded to me as if Jessie had made Isa into her accomplice—whether reading junk mags or ganging up on Connie or driving too fast in the Porsche—and it crossed my mind that Isa was now trying to figure out what I needed from her, and sub-tly adjusting herself to fit. I'd have to watch out for that.

50

Meantime, it was hard-boiling hot. Shite. I flipped and tried to float my mind out to sea, into the white noise of surf and gulls. Milo returned, shaking off water like a dog. The swim had worked up his appetite, he announced. Time for Mud Hut.

The word had gotten out. At the bar stools, we were sitting ducks. Whispers moved around us like clouds of gnats. Milo and Isa seemed aware of it. Then I saw Isa's gaze catch and hold. I followed her stare across the pool to a middle-aged workman who gripped his tackle box like it was his only friend in the world.

"Who's that?" I asked. "Why's he staring?"

"Mr. Quint." Isa took another bite of burger. "Peter's dad. We're probably just reminding him . . . of things."

Mr. Quint looked tired and defeated. His face scared me; bloated, beery, all hope lost. His red hair and blue eyes had long washed out of their youthful punch, and his freckles made a rough pattern over his skin. He'd been working on an electric panel near the cabanas, but once he'd gotten his stare out, he seemed to give us a hard mental shrug, finishing his work quickly and leaving without another look our way.

The kids had gone still. Isa spoke softly. "Poor Mr. Quint. Connie once said he'd already lost so much in his life, he couldn't afford to lose Peter, too."

"Where were Peter and Jessie going in that plane?" I asked.

Isa cast a look at Milo, who glowered. "Milo hates talking about it," she murmured. "He misses Peter."

"It's okay. Go ahead, you can tell me. It's your story, too."

"The thing is, I don't know where they were heading. Peter took Jessie's dad's plane. He'd never flown without a copilot, but he faked the paperwork."

"Was that normal, for him to do stuff like that?"

.She nodded. "Him and Jess both. They liked to dare each other into all kinds of stunts." She regarded me. "You know, it's funny how your names are both Js and how you look like her. Tall, with wavy dark brown hair. I bet Mr. Quint thought he was seeing a ghost. But I guess he's not the only one."

Her words made me tingle. So that's why there was all this extra attention on us. A dizzying thought—had Miles McRae actually chosen me for this specific reason? Since Isa couldn't have Jessie, she could have someone who looked like her? After all, I was the image of Mom; everyone said so. Maybe McRae figured any tall, cute enough, teenage brunette was as good as another.

"Why'd they end up crashing?" I asked.

Isa's eyes darted as Milo cut a swift kick her direction. "Oww-chie, Miley."

"Don't pay him any attention. Whose fault was it? Wait, Milo—" But by this point, he'd had it. He jumped off the stool and whooped to some friends on the boardwalk. Then, with a deliberate shoulder against us, he ran to chase them down. "Guess that's it for Mr. Milo." I turned to her. "I don't think he's coming back. But maybe that's better. If you still want to talk."

Isa bit her bottom lip. "Peter wasn't in radio contact. It was either engine failure or he might have gotten confused about orientation." She sat back. "I wish Miley hadn't run off. How will he get home?"

"I'm sure he'll grab a ride with friends. Nothing here seems to be too far from anything else."

"I guess I'm glad," said Isa after a minute. "I like it being just us, sometimes."

On the drive home, though, I sort of yearned for Milo's snarky presence to break up Isa's going on about who'd win in a fight, a skunk or a hedgehog. A space monster or a sea monster. A brownie or an elf. I figured she relied on babyish games to calm herself. And I sure knew how that worked. I needed some calming myself. The morning had rattled me; I thought longingly of my Ziploc and all of its treats.

"Did Peter come around the house much?" I asked as Skylark lurched into sight.

"All the time. Jessie used to say her folks are snobs," Isa answered. "Mr. and Mrs. Feathering thought Peter wasn't good enough for Jess. Peter and Jessie were like Romeo and Juliet. Have you ever seen that old movie? Starring Leonardo DiCaprio? I've seen it twelve times. It's my favorite."

"*Romeo and Juliet* was a play by William Shakespeare. Written four hundred years before Leonardo DiCaprio was born." When I cut the ignition, I saw that Isa's face was downcast. "But I bet it's a good movie, too."

"Sometimes I could see them from the lighthouse," she confessed softly. "I'd go up to spy on them kissing and stuff."

"It's creepy to spy on people," I said. "Especially when they want privacy."

"Oh, they knew. Well, Jessie knew. It was a game for her." Isa shrugged. "She thought it was funny. Jess thought everything was funny."

"And Peter?"

"He went along with her. Once Peter said they had eternal love. Too strong to die." She turned to me, her face suddenly beseeching me, her hands twisting in her lap. "Do you believe that?"

"If it was a happy love, I do," I said. "Happy love turns into good energy." Crossing my fingers that Isa wouldn't challenge my soft science on that.

Isa thought. "But Peter wasn't happy. He always said he'd make his mark one day. He wanted everyone to know he was just as smart—even smarter—than any of the summer people. Jess called him Chippy, sometimes, for the chip on his shoulder. She had names for everyone. She called me Flora, because she said I acted olden timey, like a girl from a hundred years ago."

Ha, I could see that. "Isa, what's the matter?"

"Nothing." But something was. Isa's face was tight with memory. She studied the house.

"You can tell me."

"I guess it's hard to believe every single part of Peter is dead. Especially that most extra-alive part of him that wanted to make his mark."

"Yeah, I know what you mean." Did I? Sometimes my visions of Hank and Jim remade death into a vibrant, if muted, awakening. "But I also think maybe you need to switch off your head for a while."

Inside, I made peanut-butter graham crackers.

Then, down in the family room, I found a dated, reliable romantic comedy. Life set to cute meetings and cuter music. I'd watched enough of them on my own couch at home, and it seemed like the right, mindless antidote to an overactive imagination. Isa's and mine both.

SEVEN

I'd been at Skylark for about a week when I got my first taste of a Little Bly rain.

I'd been irresponsible the night before. After staying up to watch the Fourth of July fireworks from the porch, Isa and Milo had overruled me on a horror movie that I had no stomach for, and afterward I'd put down an arsenal of meds to take me out: a sedative and then the other half of a sleeping tablet and then a new half of something else. At the rate I was going, I might be finished with the pills in less than a month, but I couldn't deal with thinking about that. I'd run across that bridge when there was no more bridge behind me. Meantime, I'd limit my intake of gory movies.

Sleep smothered me, and I woke up with a rocks-in-the-brain side effect that seemed somewhat worse than usual. The rain's fault, for sure. It had put a chill in the house, and a predictable damper on Connie's mood.

In the kitchen, I made a pot of coffee, and my decline of Connie's mandatory smoothie made her extra grumbly, as she slammed drawers and muttered about the health benefits of her rejected magical berry tincture.

"The thing is, I've got issues with blueberries," I said, which wasn't true, and half of me knew I was showing off for Milo, asserting my authority while sidelining hers.

After her breakfast, Isa got out her sketchbook and paint box to create a masterpiece from the kitchen-table fruit, while Milo escaped downstairs to play *Grand Theft Auto*. Connie shifted her complaint to lisping about her bursitis until she'd convinced herself that she'd have to spend the rest of the morning lying down. I pictured her on her back like a sea lion, wheezing and snorting. Since Connie's living quarters were two small rooms squeezed off the kitchen, at least she'd be out of my way as I tackled the house.

"I bet Skylark is over a hundred years old," I told Isa, who was blobbing a green pear into shape. "Think there's any buried treasure in here? Old letters, secret passages? Maybe we should go exploring." I hadn't had a chance to do any of that since I'd been here; Isa and Milo both enjoyed the daily predictability of Green Hill Beach, and I liked being away from Connie, and so our days had taken on a slouchy pattern. Beautiful as Skylark was, it was also like living in a museum, without so much as a slobbery dog to cozy it up. We stayed away until "theven" and then, after dinner, we watched movies down in the family room. Nights had been thankfully uneventful, too, since my first—knock wood.

But this morning, the house looked different. The rain cooled and cast shadows through every room, subtly challenging me to become a shadow myself, to flit and dart around Skylark's corners in search of its secrets.

"The house was built in 1903 by the architect Winslow Hastings Horne." Isa answered my question with the politeness of an heiress long used to being quizzed on the family estate. "Even though it's big, there's nothing very special about it. I never go exploring on the third floor. It's mostly guest rooms, and it's kind of scary—the ceilings are too high, and on a day like today, the rain pounds so hard you can't concentrate on anything else. The most interesting thing up there, supposedly, is the recamier. Dad says that one day we can sell it to pay for college since it belonged to Marie Antoinette."

"I want to see that." I had no idea what a *recamier* was. "Come on, Isa. I've been here a week and haven't bothered to check out the whole house. Let's go together."

"No, thanks. Peter and Jessie used to go up there," Isa said, but now she'd lost a touch of her "Hostess of Little Bly" voice. "And once Jessie locked me in the old playroom."

"Locked you in? What do you mean, locked you in?"

"Just what I said." But Isa had stopped painting and was twirling her paintbrush like a tiny baton. "I mean, it wasn't for a long time or anything. And she felt bad after, on account of how I threw a fit. And she gave me her best drawing to say sorry. We both love—*loved*—drawing and painting." She dunked the brush in water and began to stir. She refused to look at me, and I sensed she wanted us both to stop talking about it.

"Okay, then you keep on painting. I'll go exploring myself."

After I left, I assumed Isa'd be peeping around the corner soon enough. She struck me as the kind of girl who didn't like to miss out on a thing.

I bypassed Isa's room, a froth of pink and tulle. Appliqué butterflies alighted on several surfaces. Milo's was locked, though I bet it was identical to Teddy's inside, reeking of sweat and Old Spice while the floor was an upchuck of clothes and video games and sports equipment.

The master-bedroom suite was grand and dull, and had a deck that overlooked the sea. I imagined Miles McRae reclining in the button-back chair, reading the paper while drinking coffee that Connie'd brought up on a silver tray.

"Excellent job with Isa," he said, peering over the business section of the *Times*. "You're just as sophisticated as your mother, even if you've never summered anywhere before. I can see why Sean Ryan was attracted to you."

"Thanks," I answered. "And since we're speaking honestly, you might have mentioned that your babysitter died and your house is haunted and cursed, Miles, old pal."

But when I blinked, he was gone.

I lingered another minute, half waiting for Isa to join, and when she didn't, I took the stairs to the third floor. It was airless with the smell of cleaning ammonia and brine. Rain drummed the roof.

A softer pounding had started in my own head, and the beating rain plus no breakfast began to jumble me. My mind picked up the pattern of a Mother Goose rhyme—*rain rain go away come again another day little Isa wants to play go away ha-ha hey-hey.*

Luckily, I found a bonus stray pill in the pocket of my shorts.

I broke it between my front teeth and crushed it deep into my molars. Awful-tasting, but maybe whatever it was, it would balance me.

The first two rooms standing opposite each other were guest bedrooms, both furnished with stuffy chintz curtains and lace counterpanes. Down the hall was a storage room and Isa's unplayful playroom—*little Jamie wants to play but not the same old boring way*—with a shelf of musty fairy tales and a plastic dollhouse.

Then I entered the room that faced the playroom. Like my bedroom, it bore a thumbprint of the home's original grandeur. A canopy bed, a black marble fireplace, and voila—the recamier—an exquisitely fragile chaise lounge in faded gold brocade. Perfect for swooning.

But the room was rancid. An awful stink. I drifted through it, my fingers splayed against my nose, breathing in teacup sips. Connie's housekeeping must not extend to this floor. I practiced a swoon, diving into the chaise, and leaped up again with a scream as the pain shot into my hip.

"What the . . . ?" I found it right away, where it had dropped to the carpet. A long, heavy needle with a black bead like an evil eye on one end. Such an antique, odd-looking thing—I was pretty sure it was a hat pin. I rubbed my skin where the pin had pricked me, but as I readjusted the bolster pillow, my eyes caught in disbelief what was concealed behind it.

Crude, hard, a knife cut dug deep against the wood grain.

Its touch was rough against my fingertip, like the mindless path forged by a termite or a carpenter ant. *J* for Jessie? Strange.

Why would she have done that? If it was true that this piece of furniture had been priceless, now it was probably worth nothing. What a pointless sabotage. But I had no urge to call Connie and dime out a dead girl. I had no urge to stir up anything.

Guiltily, I replaced the pillow and then stared at it as the pinging rain seemed to beat away my thoughts *go-away go-away go-away*.

A sound drew me to the window. I parted the curtain. Through the sheet of the downpour, I saw Isa dashing toward the orchard. Someone was chasing her; I caught a flash of a gangly kid in a pink shirt and khakis who was just as quickly lost among the trees.

Milo? No. But I knew that kid.

Isa was laughing as she reappeared, streaking across the wet grass. Zigzagging around the trees through the downpour. And then the boy stopped. Lifted his head slowly to look up at the window. As if he knew I'd been watching all along. He struck a muscleman pose. To show that he enjoyed my spying on him? He was a few years older than Milo, and he wasn't as classically handsome, but he had something to him, a fierce charisma. He took a few steps closer, almost exaggeratedly, as if he were sneaking up on me, and yet his eyes were trained to a point just past me—quickly I glanced over my shoulder, to make sure nobody else was in the room. But I was alone.

I tapped on the glass, to normalize it. So that I wasn't just gawking at him. I halfway smiled.

In answer, he yawned, but from him, the gesture seemed more tantalizing, and I realized that I was standing at the very same window I'd gazed up at that first day, when Connie had picked me up and driven me here.

Only now the situation had reversed itself, and the boy was closer, almost directly below.

He was staring upward. I was looking down at him. His eyes were extraordinarily pale, a washed-out, tobacco-juice color, like those of the portrait children. And now a shiver of recognition ran down my spine as panic plucked at the root of me. My heart was racing—because yes, it was the same kid, it was the boy from the cliff, the gangly boy it was

No no no you're being paranoid. It's just some kid from next door or a friend of Milo's you're just dozy on that pill.

And then he was gone, turning away to speed around the corner of the house *friend of Milo's of course had to be*, but I jerked the curtain shut, and with that sure motion, another surprise.

Unlike the J, though, this wasn't a human endeavor. The marks that cut around the windowpane were desperate, claws and teeth that had scraped at the wood like a knife scraping corn from a cob. As if some small, feral creature had been trapped in this room, and then had tried to chew his escape through the window.

But, of course, the window had been locked. Airtight and inescapable.

A sudden vertigo spun me around as I imagined the animal's eyes on the sealed world outside. His claws scrabbling, his heart whirring. I sat on the edge of the bed *breathe deep breathe slow* and scanned the room until I found what I was looking for.

Curled in the very back of the fireplace hearth, a glove-sized lump of russet fur. The squirrel must have fallen down the chimney sometime this past winter, right into this room. Where he'd battled, lost, then crawled off to die. What a lonely end, even for a dumb, helpless creature.

Especially for a dumb, helpless creature—that's what Mags would have said. Maggie was the ultimate bleeding heart for all animals, shelter dogs and kittens and wayward spiders. If she were here, she would have insisted on a funeral. She'd want me to do something.

After a dazed minute or two, I crept across to the fireside and knelt there. The grate was blackened, the hearth thick with fresh ash and cinders. "I'm sorry, guy," I whispered. "That must have been a scary way to go."

But the smell was killing me. I had to get out.

EIGHT

"What happened to you?"

I'd returned to the kitchen, my unease refocused with the express purpose of finding Isa.

"Nothing. Have you seen Isa?"

Connie, holding a basket, was about to head downstairs to the laundry room. Her shark eyes looked suspicious. "Latht I knew, thee wath playing out in the rain without a raincoat. But what'th wrong with you? You look pale ath death."

By the view from the kitchen windows, no Isa. "If she's still out there, I should go get her and bring her in."

Turning, I saw them. *His clothes*. Pink shirt and khakis made a large, sopping wet ball on the top of the basket. My fears refreshed. "Where'd you find those?"

Connie adjusted her basket. "On the lawn. Panth might be

ruined—they're linen. Itha mutht've taken them out of her father'th clothet for dreth-up."

She spoke so matter-of-factly, as if daring me to contradict her. "Connie, didn't you see that kid out there with Isa? It wasn't Milo."

A pound of thunder made me jump as glasses rattled on the shelves. Connie was frowning. "Oh, tho now ith Milo playing in the rain, too?" A fleck of spit hit my cheek.

"I just said that it wasn't Milo. It was someone else. A skinny kid, with pale eyes and reddish brown hair."

Connie's lips pinched, but she let her laundry basket slip-slide to the floor as she blew into her hankie. "Jutht thtop. I mean it, Jamie. Whyever would you thay that? Nobody wath out there. Nobody." She crossed to the back kitchen door to send another frown through its Dutch window.

"I saw someone."

"Then you need glatheth."

"Why are you so sure I didn't?"

She turned on me, indignant, her eyes bugged, nostrils flaring and her nose the color of ham. "You think you can give me a fright, don't you? You know, you might be too much like Jethie for your own good. Everything ith funny, ithn't it? Everything ith a joke. Ath if I don't have enough to trouble me with my feet thwelled up like bread. Latht thing I need ith you trying to thcare me. Latht thing—do you hear? Between you and thith dratted rain, it'th enough to thend me back to bed till Thunday morning." And then, in a final, grand gesture, she swanned over to a high cupboard to locate a bottle of bleach, dropping it on top of the pile of dirty clothes before hauling the basket back up on her hip. Looking so self-righteous I might have giggled, if Mags had been around. Or anyone.

"Maybe Jessie thought this place needed some laughs," I said.

"Well, I am not a profethional comedian. I am a houth-keeper."

"Speaking of, there's a dead squirrel in the canopy bedroom on the third floor. He must have fallen down the chimney. He's decomposing, it's pretty gross. I guess you don't get up there much?"

"I get up there regular enough," Connie scoffed. "And I keep the chimney flueth locked tight. There hathn't been a fire built in a Thkylark hearth in yearth."

I didn't bother to comment on the fresh ashes. Thankfully, right when I needed it, my pill was beginning to soften my world. I was getting lax again, unbothered by Connie's scolding.

"But I'll go double-check," she said after another long pause, "when I get half a minute." She regarded me, the skin around her eyes winced tight. "By the way, your mother rang the houth line a little while ago. I did call for you. You better recharge your phone and call her back. Or find Itha. Whichever'th your priority."

Without waiting for my response, she turned and marched down to the basement.

After a quick ground-floor patrol—no luck—I ran upstairs, hollering Isa's name.

My cell wasn't dead. I'd just turned it off. I went to my bedroom to retrieve it. Inhaled. I knew why my mother was hounding me. This wouldn't be fun, but I'd get it over quick.

"It's me."

"Jamie! How are you adjusting? Is the job easy to handle? Is Isa a good girl?"

"Yeah, yeah. She's sweet. And it's really scenic here. Like a postcard." I looked out my window. Lighthouse. Of course. I'd bet anything Isa went there. "But, Mom, it's raining pretty hard and I need to go—"

"Then, Jamers, I guess I better cut right to it. Dad and I think someone's been into our prescriptions. Scads of pills have gone missing."

"That's odd." Hunch confirmed.

"Honey, please be honest. Did you . . . borrow . . . any of our painkillers? I need the truth here."

"Maybe I took a handful. For my back pain."

"And what about my allergy meds?"

"Oh, right, and maybe four or five of those. But Tess grabbed some of Dad's muscle relaxers for her stress fracture. I saw her with the bottle. Right before she left for Croatia."

"A lot of Dad's antihistamines are gone, too."

"Probably Tess again." My sister could handle some blame. She'd be safe at college in a couple of months anyway.

Mom, who hardly ever got mad, sounded maddish. "Those are Dad's and my own specific doctor's prescriptions. What are you girls thinking, treating our medicine cabinet like some kind of pharmacy buffet? I would never have thought my own daughters—wait, now Dad wants to say something."

As Dad's voice burred in the background. "Oh yes, sleeping pills," said Mom. "Any of those, Jamie?"

"Okay, you got me, but only two. Tess and Teddy took most. They like them for the plane trips."

66

"This is incredibly disturbing." She did sound disturbed. "Any kind of self-medicating, Jamie. It's so worrisome. Please promise me, if you *insist* on using a sleeping pill, you'll break it in half and go straight to bed. That's a narcotic, that's not a joke."

. . . *bumped my head and went to bed and couldn't get up in the morning.*

"What did you say?" Mom sounded nervous. Uh-oh. Had I said that out loud?

"My back hurts so bad it wakes me up in the morning."

"Then I'm going online this minute to look up a local doctor, and I'll make you an appointment. But if you're really having such serious issues, you need to come home—because sleeping pills are no kind of solution."

"Mom, you're overreacting. Don't make me a doctor's appointment that I won't keep."

"You just told me your back pain woke you up in the morning, Jamie. How do you think I'm going to react?"

My silence frustrated her, but there was no way she could vault the distance between us. "At the very least," she continued, "let me find you a doctor and email you the information. And we'll go see a chiropractor when you get home. *Capisce?*"

"*Capisce.*" I was off the hook, kind of. *Capisce* was one of those Atkinson family words that signaled good humor.

"Otherwise. How are you?" I could feel her listening hard.

"Me? Great."

"Wonderful." Mom sounded calmed. "And that means . . . you're not feeling too blue?"

"Blue? Like, country-western-song blue?"

"You know what I'm saying. Mopey. Down in the dumps."

"I'm fine, Mom. No blue moping in the dumps here. For real."

"Because I'm always thinking about you."

"I know. But I'm fine." I knew she wanted more. "I'm trying really hard, Mom. I'm focused on staying positive every day."

Finally, I'd said the exact right thing. "I'm sure you're a welcome addition to the McRae household," she assured me. "You're so warmhearted. That little Isa probably needs you. She's practically an orphan, poor thing."

"Sure." When it came to her kids, Mom was always selling us to us. We usually teased her about it, but after I exchanged goodbyes with my parents and clicked off, I mulled over her words.

Practically an orphan. Poor thing.

Had I once considered Milo and Isa as lonely spirits in need of my special attention? Not really. In fact, I'd hardly considered them at all. Now, in light of Mom's words, this seemed unfair of me. Sure, the McRae kids might be privileged, even spoiled, but with one deceased parent, one absent parent and last summer's plane crash like a big neon sign of tragedy blinking over them wherever they went, they'd had their share of knocks.

How surprising to be particularly needed. I'd spent these past few months barely controlling my own life. Now I'd been entrusted to care for someone else. It seemed like an absurd sort of joke on Isa and me both.

That last Ruby Tuesday lunch, Sean Ryan had sat across from me, his cherub face deflated, his blond brows knit. Keeping his distance with formal phrases like *hold on to boundaries* and *nip it in the bud* and *still want you to like me as your teacher*. He hadn't wanted to hurt me. He'd only wanted me to go away.

Just thinking about it made my face toast up.

Just thinking about it more made me want to find another pill.

"Jamie. *Jamie*. Have you gone deaf?"

Connie stood in the doorway. I hadn't heard her come upstairs. "What are you doing?"

"Me?" I looked around. We were on the third floor, in Isa's old playroom. I'd been so preoccupied that I'd wandered up here without even realizing it. "I was just looking for my shoes so I can go outside, to find Isa. I'd kicked them off earlier."

But of course my shoes weren't up here. I could feel Connie's exasperation as she followed me back down to my room. "You'd better hurry. Look what it'th doing outhide." She pointed out to the sky, dark as pewter, the rain sheeting sideways.

This wasn't just a summer storm. This was turning into a beast, and Isa might be out in it. Some babysitter-to-the-rescue I was.

"I'm leaving right now." I was already yanking my nylon orange Windbreaker from its hanger. Totally inadequate for what was raging outside, but Connie just stood there, arms crossed in her usual way, and, true to form, didn't offer me anything better.

NINE

Gusting winds drowned my voice as I released some key swears into the storm. I cursed out everyone, pretty much. The weather, Connie, even poor Mom for hunting me down and calling me out on the pill pinching. The slashing wind and angry sky agreed. But I knew that mostly I was swearing because anger was slightly more comfortable than fear.

What if something horrible had happened to Isa, on my watch? Oh Lord, I'd never forgive myself.

I started my climb to the lighthouse, working a slippery toehold, pushing uphill by way of the walkway. It was foolish to be out in a storm this electric. Surely there was an emergency number to a local patrol station I could have contacted, instead of taking on the search myself. I'd dashed out into the middle of this thing without

Crack! White veins of lightning cut the sky and struck a large tree ahead, popping it full of light like an enormous firefly.

"Isa!" I hollered. And again. Yelled her name until my throat went hoarse. The rubber thong broke off my right flip-flop, so I took them both off and threw them over the rail and out to sea. Continuing my trudge barefoot, head low, arms tucked in front of me to break my fall.

And then up ahead, there they were. My cry caught and died in me the same instant. The pale-eyed boy, the lanky girl. Both standing in position at the edge of the outcropping. Not caring about the rain, or about my presence. Whatever doubts I might have, whatever desire to pretend away what I instinctively knew, I couldn't shake the fact that in this sighting of them, they were as uncannily, as uniquely positioned as they had been the first day.

This was exactly as Uncle Jim and Hank had always appeared to me, too; as an imprint, as the lingering, unrelenting burn of a retinal afterimage. I squeezed my eyes shut into pulpy sparks of yellow and red but it was too late. They'd found me, they'd printed themselves on me, they were inside.

"You!" I yelled. I wanted their attention, even as my body zinged that I was calling to them, that I was acknowledging them at all. But there was no retreat, there was no denying it. "You!"

They couldn't hear, or wouldn't. They were turned inward on each other. I squinted through the downpour. Peter's arm moved to encircle Jessie's waist, pulling her in. Their thin, wet clothes made a cling wrap around their bodies. Her arms reached around his neck.

71

Jagged pain shot through my toe, and I howled and spun, my anchoring foot slipping on the grass, a splinter and it *hurt*, and when my gaze reconnected, I saw that, just as before, they stood hand in hand at the very edge of the cliff.

You don't exist you don't exist as I made myself walk closer to them, steeling myself to confront them, no matter that every step I took forward was a step I could have just as quickly taken back *you're nothing even if I see you so what you can't hurt anybody and so that makes you nothing it makes you nothing nothing*

And I knew they'd jump, too. Only this time I watched them—*a lover's leap,* the quaint little phrase flitted through my head—as they joined hands and then, feet churning, sailed over the edge of the cliff into the darkness below.

Once I'd reached the same point where they'd stood, I dropped to all fours and crawled on my hands and knees under the railing to stare over the cliff at the dizzying vertical drop to the rocks.

Jump. Done. Peace. The moment lured me, held me tight and tighter, transfixed me and then abruptly let me go.

They'd disappeared. Because they hadn't really been here. They hadn't even jumped *because you are dead to everyone even to me you aren't here.*

Trembling, drenched, my stupid toe throbbing, I steadied myself and scrambled back under the railing, then sprinted in the opposite direction toward the lighthouse. "Isa! Isa, answer me if you can! Are you in there?"

The door was unlocked, and I burst into the room's stone-walled silence.

She was in the corner, painting at a small iron table. She barely looked up.

"Hey, Jamie." With a nonchalant salute of the paintbrush.

"Isa, what are you doing out here? You gave me such a fright!" Still shaking, my fears now scrambled with relief that she was safe, I ran to her and flung my arms around her neck. *Practically an orphan.* "Why didn't you come back to the house when the storm got worse?"

Her face tensed. "I *did* come inside, but I heard you bumping around on the third floor and it made me . . . I don't know . . . I hate the third floor."

"So you should have gone downstairs to the family room."

She pouted. "It's private here. I wanted to see if I could paint the storm."

"And who were you running around with on the lawn earlier?" I skinned off my soaking Windbreaker, and then sat to check out the splinter tucked like a frown in my toe.

"Who?" she repeated vaguely.

It was lodged in there deep; I'd need tweezers and a steady eye, and even anticipating the project made me feel woozy. A steady eye was not my strong suit. I looked at her. "Over at Skylark, I saw some kid. Some kid you knew."

"No, I was alone," she said. "I was playing alone."

I focused her in. "You know you weren't. And it wasn't Milo, either."

Isa widened her eyes. "Who was it, then?"

"Come on, Isa, it's not a game. You can tell me."

She shook her head stubbornly. "I was all by myself."

"All right, what about out here? The kids near the lighthouse?"

"Nooo. There wasn't anybody. And I was looking out the window for a while."

So Isa couldn't see them. Or she didn't want me to know that she could see them. I wouldn't push it, though, not now.

"Let's get out of here."

"Hey, Jamie, did you see the lightning hit that tree?"

"I did."

"It's a good view from the fog bell. You should go up. Just for a minute. It's something."

"Okay, just for a minute. And then I want to get going." I didn't mind staying dry a minute or so longer, and I saw what Isa enjoyed about this place as a hideout. The round stone room was medieval but cozy, hung with bracketed lamps. A cookstove and a copper sink were tucked under a back window, and a circular staircase led up to the bell.

I took the stairs cautiously. When I got all the way to the top, the wavy glass offered a warped but breathtaking view of the sea, as well as of Skylark. It was hard to pick out too many details, but I could glimpse all the way through the drawn curtains into the canopy bedroom. Had I left that lamp on? I must have. Except that I knew I hadn't, and remembering Isa's story from the other day, about how she used to watch Jessie and Peter from this exact vantage point, I had to answer to that unrelenting tug of thought. *They were still here.* Of course they were, both of them, I knew it, had known it on some level almost from the moment I'd arrived at Skylark. The unrest of their death was defiant, it beckoned from the corners, from all of their favorite places *all their old haunts* taunting my peace of mind *pat her and prick her and mark her with a J and put her in the ocean* and if I stayed here they would

"Jamie?"

I turned with a jump. Isa had followed me, but at my sudden movement, she backed off. "Sorry." Her eyes, watchful as spiders. "Are you all right?"

"Of course. I just . . . I have a splinter in my toe. It hurts. C'mon, let's get back to the house."

"You don't like it here, do you?"

"What do you mean?" I swallowed. "Of course I do. It's beautiful. And the beach . . . it's all just so . . . great."

"Sometimes you look sad." Then, quietly, but with a sudden fervor in her voice, "Don't leave me, Jamie, please? I didn't mean it the other day, when I said that you were driving the car crazy like Jess. You're way different. I feel like you understand things about me but you're not trying to cure me, either, like Dr. Hugh."

"Isa. Chill your drama, girl. I'm not going anywhere."

"Promise?"

I went to her. Pressed my damp, cold hands against the sides of her face. "Promise, cross my heart. I am not leaving you."

But it was as if Isa knew precisely where my mind was. That I'd never wanted to leave Little Bly so much as right that moment, and despite the firm conviction of my touch and my promise, I couldn't help but resent her need, and all that I knew it would force from me.

TEN

Hours passed with no sign of Milo.

"Can I wait up for him?" Isa had been bugging me with this question all evening.

"Didn't he say he was spending the night with some friend?" I asked.

"Uh-uh." Isa shook her head. "Don't worry, I'm sure he'll show up sooner or later. Miley's got a million friends, but he always comes home to his family."

It struck me how my dislike of that kid had been crawling up on me lately. Happy as Isa had been to see him that first day, Milo seemed to do her—and me—more harm than good, what with his snobbery and wisecracks and all his subtle undermining. He was just too snide for me to get comfortable with.

And yet he wasn't going anywhere, either. Each time I'd

tentatively suggested other things Milo might do to occupy himself this summer, like maybe visit his friends in Beacon Hill, or possibly even see about tickets to Hong Kong to visit his father, Isa and Milo had both wheeled on me. They were more bonded together than I'd have imagined; it was a longtime alliance. Any attempt to separate them proved to be almost immediately frustrating.

Tonight, though, Isa seemed especially tired and needy, so I put Milo out of my mind and focused on her. Against Connie's wishes, she wanted dinner in bed, and so I ignored all the usual Funsicle grumblings as I cobbled together a tray of all my own comfort faves. Peanut butter and jelly toasties, cocoa, and a peach for dessert.

I worked to keep busy as Connie sighed about all she'd have to do to secure the house if the storm was upgraded to a hurricane, while doing not much else than fixing herself cup upon cup of Lipton. Last minute, I slapped together another PB and J toastie for myself so that I could duck the displeasure of her dinnertime company, and I ran for it.

Isa had barely finished our bedtime feast before she burrowed herself under the covers. Cocooned inside her pink butterfly room, she looked heart-achingly young and alone. *Practically an orphan.* "Will you leave the TV on?" she asked.

"How about I just turn it down?"

" 'Kay." She'd been watching *Blue Earth*. The flat screen over the mantel showed a couple of stoner koalas chewing eucalyptus leaves.

I stepped closer, using the remote to adjust the brightness. "Hey, Isa, you know there's all these tiles missing around the hearth?" They looked so ugly, gapped teeth in the blue-and-white Delft design.

"That was Peter." She yawned. "I saw him do it once. I told him I'd tell Dad. It was the only thing that made him stop."

"Why would he do it at all?"

She nestled in deeper. "Oh, Pete was always messing up stuff."

"What a joker."

"It was just his way."

I found a hearthside tile and tamped it back in. "Night, then."

"Thanks, Jessie," she murmured sleepily as she settled. I didn't bother to correct her. "Don't lock me in my room tonight, okay?"

"Of course not." Weird. How often had Jessie locked Isa in her room to keep her out of the way when Peter was over? Jessie's babysitting style officially unnerved me. Sometimes I wondered if she'd only agreed to the job so that she and Peter could have access to this house, so high and lofty on its hill, so far away from their parents' judgment.

Milo hadn't taken either of the cars, so wherever he was, he'd gone by foot. I hoped he was smart enough to stay put. I wound upstairs, pacing the corridor, and then I looped back into Isa's room, where she'd fallen asleep.

Her art notebook was drying on top of her desk.

I picked it up and flipped pages. Wildflowers, a sparrow, and then, toward the end, a sketch that had been drawn by a more sophisticated hand. A shiver lifted the hairs on the back of my neck. Now this was Jessie's work, I was sure of it. The sketch of Peter was in three-quarter view. In the taut curve of his stingray lip, I recognized that reluctant smile.

On the flip side was a drawing of Isa. She looked softer,

younger, and the date, July 5, was printed at her collar. Next to this sketch was a rendering of a hand. Jessie's hand. She'd drawn it to scale. I curled my own hand over the sketch, and now it became a near-perfect, phantom match to mine.

Last summer, Jessie was here, in love, sketching her boyfriend, driving too fast. This summer, she was gone. And yet she wasn't gone; in some ways, as long as I was here, doing all the things that she had done, an essence of her life remained trapped in this house. Or maybe in me. And in a dislocated tug of my senses, I almost missed her, even though I hadn't even known her.

Maybe my loneliness was starting to unwind me. I knew I needed more socializing than just interacting with Connie and Isa and Milo; even a daily phone call with Mags would have helped, but the longer I stuck with just myself, the more messed up I might become *rapping at the windows crying at the locks* and it was beginning to bother me how much.

"Miley's home." Isa's head snapped up like an elastic from the pillow, as if she hadn't been sleeping at all. "I think I hear him, Jamie. I bet he's freezing cold." She yawned and then, confident that on her command I'd take care of everything, dropped off just as quickly as she'd woken.

As if on cue, the front door slammed. I was downstairs in an instant.

Milo was soaked through, hair plastered and legs darkly mud-streaked. Wherever he'd been, he carried his secrets in the spark of his eyes and color in his face.

As I reached the bottom step, I crossed my arms in front of my chest and tried to do the au pair thing. "Hey. I've been worried sick."

"Hey, yourself, baby," he answered. "Glad you care."

I scooped a breath. "Where've you been?"

His smile was deliberately mysterious. "Hanging out. With my peeps."

My heart raced. He wanted me to go first. To be first to say the name. "But I know who you were out with, Milo. You were out with Peter," I whispered.

He stepped back. "Ha. One week at Skylark, and you might have officially lost your mind."

"You want to tell me, but you want to keep it private, too. I get it, Milo. That other night, when you talked about being watched?" I took the last step down. "Well, now I know what you meant. Because I saw him earlier, on the lawn. And I've seen him twice with Jessie near the lighthouse. But this isn't any news to you, because you've seen him, too, haven't you?"

Milo stared at me as if he was trying to decide something. "I need a hot shower," he said. "Maybe you haven't noticed? But it's raining." Then he charged past me up the stairs, swiping me on purpose with his wet clothes.

I followed him, up the stairs and down the hall, my words aimed at his back. "Just hear me out, okay? Because I know what it feels like. I do."

Milo stopped. Pivoted. "What *what* feels like?"

"The . . . pull." Tall as I was, I'd never been so aware of the couple of inches that Milo had on me.

"The pull," he repeated. "The pull of *what?*"

And then, in a spinning second, it was as if I didn't know him at all. As if Milo's face lost focus and his features rearranged themselves to look entirely different. What was happening? Was it the side effect of a pill? When had I taken my last pill? I couldn't remember. Blinking, I stepped to the side, my fingertips touching the wall to hold myself steady. "The pull from the other side."

This wasn't coming out right. Even in my own ears, I sounded bewildered. I wobbled on, scrabbling for my truths. "But it's a bad idea. They come to you when they sense your need. And all they want is to pull you in tighter." Saying it, I realized that this part, at least, was true. When I needed them most, I became Uncle Jim's and Hank's most electric connection to the world they'd left.

Milo shook his head hard like a dog, and in his teasing insolence, he became Milo again as the water droplets smacked across my face. I wiped them away with the back of my hand. "Okay, here's the deal, Jamie. Maybe you didn't mean it to be so random, but the last thing I need is some chick from New Jersey suddenly instructing me not to hang out with a guy who *died last year.*"

"No, Milo. *You* started this." My blood burned beneath my skin. "*You* warned me. Now I'm telling you, Peter can't be here unless you acknowledge that he is. Don't do it. The more you give in, the harder he'll hold on to you; it will be impossible—"

"And what I'm telling *you*," interrupted Milo, "is why don't you figure out how to keep your head on straight and your eyes on my sister? At least till your time here is finished. Meantime, I'll forget that we had this conversation. That work for ya?"

I swallowed. Milo's words were the hard push that shoved me outside myself.

We stared at each other. I'd been quick with my convictions, so positive that the kids on the cliff were Jessie and Peter, so certain that Milo possessed something extra special, maybe almost prophetic. I'd been sure that he'd wanted, maybe even needed, to reach out to me that first night on the porch, when he'd warned me about being watched.

I'd trusted my instinct, but I must have made a mistake. What did I have to go on, anyway? Isa hadn't ever acknowledged the kids on the cliffs. Not either day. That mark on the carpet might have been there already . . . and these stupid pills . . . I rubbed my dry eyes. I hadn't thought this out.

Milo was waiting for my response. "Okay?"

Retreat on this one, Jamie.

"Fine. Just don't come crying to me when you hear something go bump in the night." I arched an eyebrow, as if I might have been joking with him all along. My effort to preserve my dignity mortified me. Especially when, without another word, Milo shut the door in my face.

I slunk off, tunneled down to the subterranean family room, flipping from bad movies to nighttime talk shows to news programs. Just like home, only minus all my mild reassurances—Mom's voice, the woolly maroon afghan. Later, dragging myself upstairs and around the long halls toward my bedroom, I tripped against the darkness. I'd left the lamp on in my bedroom, and as I opened my door, the light spilling out into the hall seemed to ignite my vision.

The children had changed. I sensed it even before I turned to confront the portrait head-on. They were watching me now, with held breath and three sets of eyes. Two boys and their sister, posed exactly as they had always been. Navy velvet, tatted-lace collars, strawberries-and-cream complexions. Then what was different? Was it their expressions that had altered, or my perception?

Slowly and methodically, I made myself step forward. My fingers reached out to touch the canvas, tracing lightly across the bumpy, cool surface, passing over the older boy's cheek and up to his eye, the center of his pupil, where a tiny hole had been stabbed clean through. I could feel the rough notch of its split against my fingertips.

I touched the other eye. Same. Both eyes of every single child had been punctured through the center. More than a pin, less than a fork. So precise as to be undetected.

Almost undetected.

Stepping back, I was conscious of a dull roar, as if I were holding a conch shell to each of my ears.

It was hardly any change, and yet for all intents, it had mutilated the children. They had become eerie distortions of themselves. My heart tumbled as I stepped back to look at the portrait again. Now that I'd discovered it, there was no way not to see it.

"You think you're so sly, Peter," I spoke low into the darkness, my own voice soothing me, reminding me that I was here, truly here, in a way that he was not. "But I don't. And now I'm learning your tricks, aren't I?"

Of course, I wasn't the first person who had discovered them.

ELEVEN

Just by luck, I was able to broach the topic with Connie the very next evening. Milo had gone out with friends, while Isa had been invited by a Green Hill Beach Club family to a barbecue. Since Connie had already bought groceries, she went ahead with dinner. She liked to eat, I'd noticed, and devoted much time to shopping for, preparing and cleaning up meals. It tired me just to watch.

But tonight I decided to help with the salad—a first—which seemed to make her happy. Or at least she was humming as she brushed a marinade onto the tuna steak that she was preparing with tomatoes and capers. When I hauled out the full trash bag to the Dumpster, she thanked me—another first.

The Dumpster was tucked back along the hedgerows. As I yanked it open, dirty collected rainwater sloshed down my legs, and a flock of flies swooped up in my face.

"Ecchh!" I batted them away. Connie had tucked the dead squirrel into a wastepaper bag, but she hadn't knotted it right. I chucked it into the garbage bag and slammed down the lid, then raced back up to the house.

Connie had set the table. She said grace. Then we ate in silence.

"Pretty day at the beach," I started. "They had some competitions today, and Isa placed third in her division for diving."

"Mmmph." Not a great jumping-off point, so to speak. Connie wasn't much for activities; she seemed to much prefer the Great Indoors.

"I love how you did the zucchini," I said, smiling, hoping I didn't seem too not-me.

"Wath a time Itha wouldn't eat anything until I pureed it," Connie remarked as she ladled me a second helping. "Thpoiled children can be a challenge and a trial. I grew up on the island. We all hated thummertime, when the fanthy folk came in. I'm thtill thuthpithuth." This last word would have set Mags off; alone, I nodded seriously.

"But aren't the McRae people fancy folk?"

"I work for Thkylark," Connie clarified. "And my mother before me, and her mother before her. And *her* mother lived here. Thkylark wath built by my great-grandfather."

"Winslow Hastings Horne?"

Connie looked pleased. "Why, how do you know 'bout him?"

Here was my opportunity. A pleased Connie was not in her signature mood. "My parents are architecture buffs," I lied. "I read about Horne in one of their books. He's kind of a big deal. In my house, anyway."

Pleasure opened Connie's face. "He'th internationally

recognithed. Fact ith, I own Horne's only thilhouette." She leaned forward. "Never published."

"Horne's silhouette? Cool. I can't wait to tell my parents." I gave it my all. "So you're from an original family of Bly."

Connie seemed thrilled that I'd reached this conclusion on my own. "That'th true."

"And the Quints have lived here forever, too, right?"

Another nod. "Augie Quint doeth home thecurity. He can lock and unlock the entire island with the touch of a button."

"Was Peter planning to go into the family business?"

Connie's lips pursed at the name. "Peter? No . . . too much of a hothead."

"But he sounds like he was fun to be around."

A tic in her face suggested doubt. "He'd come over full of mithchief. Throw Itha in the air, tell joketh, play all hith awful muthic real loud. But he brought in the dark, too."

"What do you mean?"

She hesitated. "Moody, wath all I meant."

"And Jessie? What was she like?"

"A thummer Bly girl. Only thing different being how thee picked Peter over her people—and her family weren't none too happy about that." Connie pulled out her hankie and blew.

"But it must have been hard on Peter."

"How tho?"

"Just, I mean, with Jessie and Isa and all these other Bly kids having so much." It was now or never. "I've been here over a week. And I've discovered some things. The strange things he did."

"Who?"

86

"Peter. I've noticed how he took some of his, you know, his darkness out on Skylark."

"What are you thaying?" If Connie'd had quills, they'd all have been sticking out in defense.

"Almost like little tantrums or grudges." I shrugged. "Even Isa knew about it. It's like there are all these scars all over the house."

Connie fell quiet.

"Like the cigarette burns." Now I'd really launched myself. "And the missing tiles in Isa's fireplace. I know you saw the J that he knifed into the wood of that lounge chair upstairs. At first I'd thought it was Jessie, but that's not her style at all. She was outgoing, a free spirit. He was different, more withdrawn, but he was angry, too—and he's done a lot of damage around here. That's why you never go up to the third floor, right? Because you take good care of this house, Connie. You see everything. Except for some reason you've decided not to see the pinholes in that portrait of the three kids. And you've ignored the ashes in the fireplace, and the dead squirrel and the—"

"No, no, thith ith all too thilly." With a snap of her head, Connie seemed to break herself from her trance of listening. "I don't have the leatht idea what you mean," she declared.

"You do so," I pressed. "You let Peter hang out here all last summer. Because he was a local, and the locals always watch each other's backs. But you didn't know the damage he was doing, or you'd never have let him. You're probably still kind of upset about it, since it all happened on your watch, am I right?"

Hot spots had appeared in her cheeks. The flat of her hand rolled her napkin back and forth, back and forth. It made me nervous to see her so vulnerable. I'd expected something else: a guilty admission, and an alliance, maybe. "Go tell the Mithter, then," she said stiffly. "If it'th trouble you've wanted all along."

"But I don't want anything." I shook my head, my voice suddenly thinning on me as I entreated her. "I'm trying to understand what's going on in this house, too, that's all. I'm . . . I'm on your side." Was that true? It seemed true.

Connie's hands were vein-corded and liver-spotted; they made me feel sorry for her in a way that the rest of her didn't. And I could see that my last words had hit their mark. She paused. Then seemed to decide something as she stopped playing with her napkin and brought her hands under her chin, her eyes unfocused. "I go over it in my head, over and over, but I jutht don't know why he did it. Like the way thome people pull a dog'th tail or pinch a baby. Peter liked to pick at Thkylark. I didn't thee the half of it until he wath gone. Even now. Theemth like I'm alwayth dithcovering thomething new."

"Connie"—I spoke carefully—"that's because he's still doing it."

Abruptly, she shoved up from the table. "*Now* you're talking blathphemy." She angled a finger at me, all trace of her earlier good humor collapsed. "I don't need any more from you, Jamie. With my own eyeth, I thaw that boy'th cathket laid in at Thaint Bartholomew latht Aughust, not five mileth up the road. With my own eyeth!" She bugged them out, turning herself grotesque, and then snatched up my unfinished dish and whisked past me to the kitchen sink.

"There's a presence here," I insisted. "His, mostly. If she's here, it's only through what she meant to him. But he's angry and I can feel him. From the very first night, I could."

Connie was jerking her head like a bee was circling it. "Enough, enough. I'm a woman of faith. I don't believe in anybody come up from the earth to haunt it. You're talking pure nonthenth." Then she yanked on her rubber gloves with all the grandeur of heading to the opera, and made an equal production of turning on the faucet taps.

But if I'd been talking *pure nonthenth*, then Connie wouldn't have reacted so strongly. Instead, she was attacking the dishes as if they needed to be purged of their sins. As if she could scrub off our conversation with her bristles and detergent.

"It would be better if we were together on all this," I said. "You sense it, too, Connie. It's not fair to me to pretend that you don't."

But now she'd morphed into full-on madwoman, muttering and shaking her head at her soap bubbles. Evidently, she wasn't speaking to me anymore. Not about this, anyhow. Yet I'd flustered her because I'd hit a nerve. Her reaction was her confession. Maybe she couldn't detect Peter and Jessie like I could, but she knew. Meantime, I was faced with her thorny mood and the slap of the dishwater.

So I left her, scooting downstairs to my refuge: the family room, where the babble of the television always seemed to temporarily banish whatever else was trapped inside these walls.

TWELVE

Awful as it would have been to admit it to him, I heeded Milo's advice. I took care of Isa, and tried to forget his and my harsh exchange. And Isa by herself—as in, Isa not working to impress her big brother—could be a delight. Soon I'd stopped worrying about whether or not I was sinking too deep into her world of corny "what if" games. They all seemed pretty harmless to me.

But Dr. Hugh probably would have invoiced a different diagnosis, so we made a point to duck Connie's watch. I was sure Mags would have died laughing to see me paddling around in the pool or ocean pretending to be an Olympic swimmer, or instructing a "studio audience" how to make honeydew-melon sorbet. But Mags wasn't here. Just Isa and me and an endless radiance of sunny days—and it wasn't all that bad.

Except that even Isa had friends her own age. And as the

drift and spin of days made weeks, I was getting downright desperate for some of my own. Blyers had proven to be way less "kick-back" than Miles McRae's email suggested. Most other au pairs were swanky summer kids, like Jessie. The more I looked around, the more apparent it became that I was a rare breed here: the unknown import.

One of the Green Hill Beach Club lifeguards that everyone called Noogie had been nicest to me. Since Isa had signed up for advanced diving lessons, I saw Noogie every day. We'd say hello, and then I'd study her from behind my book. There was something about her. She was pretty in an athletic way, like Mags, and she was unsuckuppy with parents. Everyone, myself included, liked to be around Noogie, just listening to her laugh and joke and banter with the kids. She reminded me a lot of Tess and Teddy, themselves both extroverts. Watching Noogie, I missed the twins, and dreaded thinking of next year: the empty rooms, the quiet threesome of me and my parents. I'd already experienced a taste of it this past spring since Tess and Teddy had never been home, wrapped up in senior week and prom and graduation.

And then, just like that, it happened. One afternoon, Noogie, on break and ambling back from the Mud Hut, dropped down to the empty lounge chair beside me.

"Why are you always staring at me?"

Humiliated, I blinked down at my book. "I'm not."

"Is it payback because we always stare at you?"

When I looked up, she was smiling ruefully. "I'm sure you know by now how much you look like her."

"And that is so not my fault."

Noogie's laugh was more like a bark. *Arf, arf.* Her trademark, husky laugh that was part of her coolness. "Fair enough. But did Miles hold a contest and you won it? The 'who looks the most like Jessie Feathering to scare the bejesus out of everyone at Green Hill' contest?"

I straightened. "Listen, this whole situation was news to me, too. Until a month ago, I didn't know Little Bly existed. And I was totally ignorant that certain beaches in the USA came equipped with valet parking and personal cabanas."

Which made Noogie bark-laugh *rough, rough, rough* all over again. "Green Hill's not bad, if you don't happen to resemble the girl who had your job last year. If Jessie were here today, she'd have thought it was hysterical."

"Except it's not."

"True." Noogie grew instantly sober. "And Miles McRae is no father of the year." Then she lowered her voice, though Isa was all the way on the other side of the pool, practicing her jackknife. "He's so checked out, he probably thought he was doing something nice, finding a . . . doppelganger—to take Jessie's place. Uh-oh—hang on."

I looked around. Out of the corner of her eye, Noogie'd caught a splash fight. Her lifeguard's whistle pierced the air. "Molly! Jonas! Out of the pool."

As they climbed out, culpable and defiant, Noogie returned her attention to me. "So, tell me. How's it been so far?"

"The job? It's okay. I get to sleep in. And Isa's a snap."

"Yeah, but Isa's also, like, eleven. Why don't you come party with us tonight?"

"Sure." I said it too quickly. Loserishly.

Noogie didn't seem to mind or care. "Sweet. My brother,

Aidan, will get you when he picks up his girlfriend, Emory—she lives close by you. Say, sevenish. Mrs. Hubbard can babysit. *Connie*," she clarified, seeing my puzzlement. "But to all us lifers, she's Mrs. Hubbard."

"What's a lifer?"

"Someone who's been coming here every summer since forever. But don't confuse us with the locals who live at Bly year round. Or tourists, who are just trying on the island for size. Not that a pureblood local like Mrs. Hubbard splits hairs between lifers and tourists."

"Now that I think about it, asking Connie, I don't know . . ."

"Oh, come on, that's what she's there for. Jessie only worked days—and it's not like you're interfering with Mrs. Hubbard's nightly tango practice down at the dance hall. She's just sitting around; she can keep one eye on Isa and the other on her wine—no problem."

Which made me smile, since one glass of wine was Connie's drink of choice. I could never get over how Little Blyers all knew one another's business. But still I held out, imagining Connie's miffed reaction as I asked her to babysit Isa while I went off to have fun at a party.

Noogie gave my arm a small pinch. "What are you supposed to do? Keep a little girl and an old lady company every single night? Watching sitcoms and helping out with the newspaper word jumble?"

Again, it was so exactly what had been happening—except that Isa watched nature programs, and Connie did sudoku, not the jumble—that now I laughed outright. "Okay, okay. You obviously know exactly how my summer's working out so far."

Noogie dropped her sunglasses over her eyes and stood up.

"But that's about to change. I guess I'm your fairy godmother. See you tonight."

"Yep." And she left, stopping half a dozen more times to chat with other kids and moms and friends before climbing up onto her lifeguard chair. Noogie really did seem to have almost magical properties. At least, she'd made one of my wishes come true. I'd get to leave the house tonight. Finally. Hooray.

THIRTEEN

For the first time since I'd arrived at Bly, I dipped into some of my cuter clothes, the ones I'd hung up in the closet rather than tossed into drawers. Did Little Bly kids get done up, or did they keep it basic? Jeans or the capris? Finally, I went simple, a washed-to-eggshell-blue cotton sundress with a boat neck and spaghetti straps. A dress, not dressy.

"I could always tell when Jessie'd been out late the night before." Milo had startled me. He was slouched in my bedroom windowsill, a resigned smirk playing on his lips, like when Sean Ryan had been about to give us the results of a chem test we'd all failed.

"Really, how?" I asked, careful to keep the curiosity from my voice.

"She'd yawn and drink a dozen cups of coffee and ignore Isa."

"Have some faith." As I moved through to the bathroom, I rumpled his hair in a way that I hoped was just a touch condescending, and he snapped his head away, then jumped and moved toward the fireplace out of reach. "Aha, so you're upset?"

"It won't be any fun."

"Let me judge that. Who knows, maybe tonight's the night I find my soul mate."

"Ha. Not here you won't, Jersey Girl. Besides, I think Isa really wants you to stay and watch *The Sound of Music* with her."

"She won't suffer to watch it with Connie." I was in the bathroom now, blotting and removing my makeup. Even a tiny amount now seemed way too New Jersey. Score one for Milo; he'd done his job dismantling my confidence.

"You sure you're ready to handle it?" he called from my room. "Just from my impression, you seem kinda rustic for them. Not to offend you."

Rustic? My mascara wand stopped in midair. Was that true? Or was he teasing, looking to get a rise out of me? "I'll try not to pick my teeth with a knife. And by the way, that comment puts you deep in brat turf."

I could hear him continuing to pace my room. My inclination was to shove him out, but instead, I finished my lashes and moved to gloss. I was debating whether I should pinch a pill for the road when the sound of the car grinding its way up the drive outside made me jump. I whipped my cardigan off the bathroom hook and scampered downstairs.

Half scared that they'd leave without me. I had cabin fever pretty bad.

Milo followed. He didn't answer when I called out goodbye.

Just thudded down the steps, nearly knocking into me in order to join Isa.

Twilight etched a silver luminescence through the trees. I stepped outside at the same moment that Aidan McNabb swung out of a sleek black Lexus convertible. A preppy vision in a golf shirt and madras shorts, he was a thicker, more freckly version of his sister.

"Hey. Jamie, right? I've heard a lot about you," he said. "Glad you're joining us tonight." His eye roved me, appraising. I tried not to care, but I didn't like it.

His girlfriend waved through the passenger window. "Hi, I'm Emory." She was a stylish beauty with salon-streaked hair and matching chunky gold jewelry, so neatly presented that I kind of wished I'd run Connie's hot iron over my sundress.

As I slid into the backseat, I saw Connie on the porch. I leaned out. "Thanks for the night off, Connie." Ever since our dinner together, I felt like she'd taken just as many pains to avoid me as I had to stay off her grid. Obviously, those things I'd said about Peter still upset her. We'd never discussed it again.

But she *was* taking over my babysitting job tonight. So she couldn't be too mad.

"Bye, Mrs. H.," chorused Aidan and Emory. I buckled up and closed my eyes. While every particle of my being wanted to push out and away from Skylark, the prospect of this night of all new people gave me jitters. Milo's undermining hadn't helped any.

Oops—and I hadn't remembered a pill. Shite. I hoped my back didn't spasm and ruin everything.

"Old Mother Hubbard," Aidan said. "Bet you're glad to lose her for a while."

"You said it." But I didn't want to come down too hard on Connie. I got a feeling that while the lifers made fun of her, they also liked her. Connie was what people tended to call "local color" and "a character"—which really meant that off this island, she'd be a complete social reject, but as long as she was here, she was landmark protected.

What impelled me to open my eyes just then? To twist around in my seat and look back at the house? Was it the feeling of being watched? That ancient need to confront the watcher?

I knew the kids were both down in the family room. Connie was standing out on the porch. And the figure was exactly where it had been the first time, observing everything from the third floor.

There, then gone, as we bumped down the drive and turned out onto Bush Road, though my heart continued to pound as my restless fingers discovered a pill nestled roly-poly in the corner of my dress pocket. Aha. Fantastic. At least I had that. A pill, any pill, seemed to do wonders in terms of blurring my relationship with everything, including Skylark, turning it irrelevant and shrinking it to pretty-postcard distance. Twenty minutes into almost any pill, I'd feel that numb, dozing, less "me" feeling ease my grip, giving me space to zone out and breathe easy.

But would Isa be okay? The thought hurt as it caught and lassoed me back to reality.

Of course she would. She had Connie, who had probably already taken her newspaper puzzle and her single glass of wine downstairs to settle in for a night of Julie Andrews. And I had to get out of here. Even if this one night out was a total bust, I couldn't deal with another evening of Skylark lockdown.

"Where's this place, the Rickrack?" I asked.

"It's where the party's at, darling," said Emory, in that tone pretty girls often used—self-confident but on the boundary line of snotty.

"Woo-hoo!" Aidan turned up the music as I forced myself to leave my doubts behind, and I tested a laugh into the wind.

FOURTEEN

"Punch?"

We hadn't been in the club for more than a minute when the guy stepped out of the shadows. He was offering me a hollowed human skull brimful of a bloody-red liquid and topped with a straw and a paper umbrella.

"Oh. Thanks." I took the skull—plastic—from the guy, whose sudden, wide Hollywood smile broke the serious expression of his face. He nodded acknowledgment while reaching past me to hand another skull punch to Emory.

"*Merci*, babe," she said.

"Out back." He jabbed his thumb.

We made a bumbling train, me following Emory, who followed Movie Star Teeth, with Aidan behind me, no doubt checking out my butt, and all of us winding through the blue-lit space.

The walls throbbed with a deconstructed reggae riff of an old Bowie song; a series of paneled screens around the bar showed a flickering tennis match where a Williams sister was clearly dominating.

I inhaled the warmth of salt air, weak beer and cigarettes—the heady fragrance of a beach party, like the ones Mags and I went to when we road-tripped to Avalon. I could feel myself loosen into the warm swing of the night. If only Mags were with me. But *at the very least,* it was happening, it was here and now, and it was definitely good enough.

From the clamshell claustrophobia of inside, we spilled from the back door onto a wide-planked platform terrace where about a dozen kids were camped at a table made from pushing two picnic tables together.

"That's us," said Aidan. He'd put his hand on the small of my back. Firmly.

Noogie was presiding. "Jamers, I was scared you'd bail!"

I smiled and sipped at my skull through a straw. Shyness, along with this tricky business of Aidan's unwanted attention, had 'stolen my vocabulary. Did Emory see what was going on? And what should I do about it? Time for that pill. I popped it and chased it with the mystery drink, which tasted as innocent as Isa's lemonade, though I knew it probably wasn't.

"Everybody, meet Jamie!" Aidan proclaimed. As I sat, he settled next to me with a proprietary air. His body language had me on high alert; it was way too close, too touchy, too sure of himself and of my favorable opinion of him. "She's the McRae au pair this summer."

Skulls were raised. Fingers fluttered.

GREENFIELD PUB LIBRARY
5310 W. LAYTON AVENUE
GREENFIELD, WI 5322 0

I fluttered mine back. "Hi, everybody." I'd done my hair twisted up, with some pieces flat-ironed, and I'd made my eyes smudgy with a bare touch of bronze eyeliner. A deliberate mask to distinguish me from Jessie Feathering—who, in the cell-phone snaps Isa'd showed me, had usually kept her lips red and her hair styled in loose, wavy layers. Nevertheless, I got the usual double takes.

Movie Star Teeth had dropped to sit on my other side. Excellent. I'd focus concentration on him, and maybe Aidan would leave me alone. My bones were unhinging, my muscles relaxing. The pill already? No, but definitely the idea of the pill was at work.

"So, I don't get it. What's the theme of this club?" I asked Teeth. "Do skulls with umbrellas mean Hawaii? Or pirates?"

"Never thought about it." He made a pose of looking serious. "Yeah, the Rickrack might be a Hawaiian theme. Like, Rickrack, God of the Pineapples. But then of course there's the famous pirate, Cap'n Jack Rickrack."

"Of course." I laughed. Laughing felt good—it deflated my anxieties. We kept going, making stupid pirate sounds and overplaying lamely off the joke while not wanting to give it up.

"Sebastian, I've never seen you act so friendly," remarked Emory.

"Because when I'm not acting, I'm not acting," said Sebastian.

Emory made a face. "You theater geeks are *always* acting."

"Not true," said Noogie to me. "Sebastian's middle name is sincerity."

Sebastian raised his skull. "It's actually David, but I'll sincerely drink to that."

102

While Sebastian did seem different from the other guys in this crowd, I couldn't hone in on exactly why. His soft bristle of dark-blond hair wasn't trying to be fashionable, in the trendy, Little Bly guy style of flopped in the eyes or tucked ragged behind the ears. He didn't care about clothes, either; his threadbare cottons fell comfy against his sinewy body.

Maybe that was it. Sebastian was no-frills. No belt, no cap, no surfer-dude necklaces, only an economical-looking sports watch. There was one surprise, in that his left inner forearm all the way to his wrist was scarred in a welted crosshatch. It was easily visible, but he didn't seem at all self-conscious about it.

Sebastian's biggest extravagance was his smile, I decided, and he sure didn't throw it around. He might have Movie Star Teeth, but they didn't accessorize a Movie Star Personality. In fact, the opposite. I wanted to talk to him more, but he'd turned away, diverted by a comment that spun into a conversation with a redhead named Lizbeth who was on his other side. She, and the others, had a lot of nicknames for Sebastian, including Bass, Sibby and Brooks—which I took to be his last name.

It was obvious that kids really liked this guy, to the point where they vied and jousted against one another for his attention. As much as I wanted to join in, I decided to take the laid-back route, and so I swiveled into listening to Aidan's recap of his entire day at his landscaping job, which mostly entailed helping cranky old Mrs. Grosvenor, who'd made him haul a dozen rosebushes all around her garden before deciding she didn't want them. It was kind of a funny story, except that the person most entranced with its humor was Aidan, which somewhat deflated my enjoyment of it.

"So, Jamie, tell me something." Emory, seated directly across, had been looking at me. Now she leaned closer in, pitching her elbows in my direction so we could speak more privately. "What's your take on Isa? I taught her tennis last year. Or tried to, anyway. She was pretty hopeless with the hand-eye coordination."

"She's an excellent swimmer," I said, probably too defensive.

"But she's an odd duck. She's got a major case of la-la land, don't you think?"

"Well, she has a great imagination."

"No doubt. Sometimes that girl could make me feel like *I* was the freak," said Emory, shaking back her hair and smiling as if this thought were so ridiculous it could hardly be imagined. "Just because I couldn't see the people in her world. It's lucky she's grown up here, around all of us who've known her since she was teeny."

"My friend Maggie and I were goofy kids, too," I confessed. "In fact, Isa and Milo seem fairly normal, considering the circumstances."

"Uh-oh." Emory's perfect eyebrows angled skeptically. "Milo's back?"

I nodded. "He left camp early. It's no big deal. We hardly ever see him. Honestly, it's a good thing. It makes Isa happy to have her big brother again. Obnoxious as he can be."

Emory primmed up her mouth as she shook her head. Not a Milo fan, either. "Yeah, sure, right. She used to try to make me play tennis with him. For me, Milo's always been a pest who's best left ignored. You're cool to handle it."

"Not everyone would," said Aidan, his leg a sudden, intimate pressure against mine; it startled me. "But then again, you've got a lot of Jessie's light."

"Aidan, c'mon, you're such a flirt. Don't scare the girl," said Emory. Her voice had gone tense with disapproval.

She didn't know the half of it. Or maybe she did. The look she gave me was complex: a flash of female-to-female understanding that was just as quickly weighted with frustration, and then defaulted back to cool-girl indifference.

Quickly I slid a couple of inches away from Aidan. Even though it nudged me closer to Sebastian, who was getting a lot of breathy laughs out of Lizbeth. They'd been talking a long time. Were they going out? What was the deal? I couldn't get a handle on it.

Worse than this, though, was my creeping-crawling realization that something strange was happening to me. A fuzz in my vision, and the unreasonable sense that I was five seconds behind every joke. As I laughed and sipped my drink and tried to appear as comfortable and appropriate as I could, I'd started to panic. My fingers squeezed the skin of my upper thigh, as if I could pinch myself back into my senses.

"Everything good?" Sebastian asked as he finally turned.

"Uh-huh." But when I blinked, his face became a double image, two pairs of eyes peering at me intently as a blackbird *and wasn't that a dainty dish to set before the king.*

"You sure?"

"Mmm." I thought of Sebastian flying out of a pie and I wanted to laugh. But that wasn't funny. Something was wrong. I looked around the table. Voices were gummy vowels. Mouths appeared cavernous, and the collection of skulls on the table had come to life, eyeless eyes on me, trembling in a disembodied dance.

Which pill had I chosen? What was I drinking? *Idiot idiot idiot.*

" 'Scuse me," I mumbled as I stood up. Tried not to make eye contact with Sebastian, or anyone else, as I swerved back into the club. My hand trailing the wall for support, until I managed to find the restroom. It was packed, fluorescent, too much.

I veered out again, my hand on the wall.

What had I taken? Not a sleeping pill. And yet I felt a chilling certainty that, yes, a sleeping pill was exactly what I'd swallowed. I remembered the last time I'd worn this sundress, about a month ago, during a drive-by of my parents' bathroom. I'd sneaked out a sleeping pill from Mom's supply. Hoarded it as ammunition against the next roaming, restless night.

Maybe I could stick my finger down my throat and vomit it up? I'd never done anything like that before. My relationship with food was normal—the whole freshman-year faux-bulimia craze had passed me by entirely.

But the air was too stuffy for me to think, and I was getting nauseous—with apprehension? From the pill?

If this pill was potentially going to mess me up, I needed to bust out some decisions, fast.

"Jamie?" Sebastian had come out of nowhere. "You all right? I came to find you."

"I am, thanks. Something I drank. Must've gone down the wrong way." I propped a shoulder against the wall. "And it's just too, um, crowded in the girls'."

"We're right on the dunes, you know." Sebastian swept out his hand. "Nature's call can take you to nature. Come on. Outside. I'll stand watch."

"Oh." He'd laced my fingers through his. "Okay."

With Sebastian leading, we sneaked out a side exit and into the night, meandering along the boardwalk to where the dunes lumped across the starry horizon.

"Up there." He pointed. "But I'll stand guard down here. Watch out for pincer crabs."

I stopped.

"Kidding, I kid." He smiled. "You're cute when you're scared."

"I was thinking . . . you're cute when you smile."

"We're a pair of cuties, huh." He gave me a nudge. "Holler if you need me."

I knew he could tell that my equilibrium was off. But I stepped forward, pigeon-toed and buckle-kneed, through the sand. As the cool air flowed into my lungs and over my skin, my nausea eased. Throw up, no. But pee, oh yes. Though under normal circumstances, the idea of squatting so near a cute guy, in an open space, would have sent me up a tree with anxiety. On the other hand, these were not normal circumstances. I'd never tried to stay awake on sleeping pills before. It didn't feel good. Not at all.

Mission accomplished, I picked my way back toward Sebastian, nearly falling on him. His hand shot out to steady me.

"Careful. Looks like you've got a minor balance issue."

"Maybe slightly."

"Want to stay out here a minute? We can check the horizon for pirate ships."

"Sure." I gulped oxygen and didn't give in to the hazy, addled impulse to rest my hand on one of Sebastian's muscle-knotted quadriceps.

The last time I'd sat so intentionally close to a male was when Sean Ryan and I had met at Maggie Moo's for sundaes. We hadn't called it a date. But we'd sat close, on that bench, in that mall, on the other side of town. *It had meant something no it hadn't forget it forget it forget it.*

"You're looking at me funny."

"Sorry." I felt terribly, tremendously bashful. "Didn't mean to."

"You sure you're doing okay?" Sebastian let his hand rest a moment on my shoulder.

"Uh-huh." *Change subjects.* "So, are you a lifer or a local?" I asked.

"Guess."

"Local?"

"Reason?"

I considered it. "Somehow I don't see you as a golf caddy or a tennis coach. In the perfect shorts and perfect pair of sunglasses."

Sebastian laughed. "Good call. Yep, I'm a local boy, born and raised in Bly. As for a summer job, you'll find me six days a week busting my butt down at Sunrise Dry Cleaners—my parents own it. It's real money, and I need it. I've got a scholarship to Yale to study drama that pays exactly one dollar more than not being able to swing it at all. Which I've heard is how most scholarships tend to work."

"Yale. That's impressive."

"I'm selling too hard." He made a face. "I know you for ten minutes, and I go and college-drop. Maybe I still have to say it out loud to believe it."

"Hey, Yale's a huge deal. And you're rocking a scholarship."

"You think I'm That Guy Who Brags."

"Not at all."

"It's okay; I probably *am* bragging. On that, maybe I don't own the perfect pair of sunglasses, but I do have a couple of incredible pairs of driving goggles."

"Driving—*what?*" I laughed.

"You'll see." He tapped two fingers to my nose, an offhand

gesture that dizzied and thrilled me. "See, now I'm attempting to be fascinating yet cryptic. Instead of braggartly. Wait—is that a word?"

By now we were both laughing. "Oh, definitely *braggartly* is a word. I use it all the time."

"This is new for me."

"What is?"

"Wanting to impress someone."

"I'm flattered." I really was. "But why me?"

"I don't know. I like that you're an exotic stranger instead of someone who's shown up on this island like clockwork every single summer for the past fifteen years. I like how you bite your bottom lip when you listen. Mostly I liked watching you give Aidan McNabb the stone-cold shaft. He's the crown prince of Bly, and he's not used to the swift kick of rejection."

"He's met his match. I'm not into that guy, and I'm not afraid to kick."

That was all he needed. Without another word, Sebastian leaned forward and kissed me.

My last kiss had been courtesy of Sean Ryan—only once, in the furtive winter dark, in his icy Mini Cooper. Sebastian's mouth was different. Careful, the way he cupped his hands against either side of my face as if I were something divine and limited being offered to him. But confident, the way he shifted himself so that my hands found his shoulders, and then wrapped around them, as I sensed his entire mind and body focused on me and nothing else.

But the surprise of it, plus the scramble of the sleeping pill in my brain, also conspired in the worst way possible as my nervous laughter burbled from my throat and *ulp*ed into the air.

"What's funny?" As he drew away, the question held his uncertain smile.

Now I couldn't stop giggling. "Nothing. I'm drunk . . . maybe."

"Nah, you're not drunk. You had three sips of rum punch, and I happen to know that the bartender, Harry, who's also my cousin, is watering the cocktails to criminal levels."

I was silent.

"Not sure why I kissed you," Sebastian admitted into the pause. "I was pulling for leading man, but I might have come off as an unintentionally comic sidekick."

"No, I liked it. Really. It was bold." But he still looked unsure.

I wanted to say the perfect thing so Sebastian would know how much I'd wanted him to kiss me, but without seeming too extreme about it. "It's just that I'm not myself tonight," I said thickly. Stupidly. My brain was going into Tilt-A-Whirl. I was losing ground, fast, on this situation.

"Copy that," he answered softly.

"In fact, to be honest, I'm starting to feel awful."

He stood. "Got it." Offered a hand to help me up. "Let me take you back to Skylark."

FIFTEEN

Sebastian drove a motorcycle. It looked like nothing I'd seen before.

"A Triumph Bonneville T120," he explained. "Otherwise known as Bonnie. She's about fifty years old."

"Sweet." It was a pretty bike, slender and compact. "So is this where your driving goggles come in?"

"You're quick, detective." He opened the seat and pulled them out, along with a couple of vintage leather helmets. He then carefully fit goggles and helmet onto my head, adjusting the eye and chin straps.

"I feel like Amelia Earhart. Or maybe Snoopy." I yawned. "Snoopy, Dopey, and Sleepy."

He peered at me. "Hold on tight, and I'll get you home slow and safe."

"Yessir."

We left the club in a roar. The open breeze kind of woke me up and made me feel better. I tied my arms around Sebastian's waist and leaned forward to press against his back. My jumbled mind hummed nursery rhymes, and my hands held a locked grip at his waist; I was terrified that my body would spontaneously go limp as the pill continued to sneak its way through my system.

We rounded the bend, off Bush Road, and then up the drive, the tires grinding sand as Sebastian downshifted. Midway, the bike sputtered, and I thought we'd lost traction. Quickly, Sebastian rose up and pushed his weight over the handlebars. The engine growled and the wheels spun and coughed like a tired beast, and then we shot up the hill in a jet of speed and noise that I figured would wake up everyone.

But the house stayed dark. Sebastian cut the engine and we got off. I pulled free of my heavy helmet and goggles. My head felt mushy as an overripe melon. I wished I could slice it open and let the sleeping pill ooze out like syrup. And I didn't want to go inside the house.

"This has been such a strange experience," I blurted.

"You mean Bonnie? She looks delicate, but she's fairly durable. But I gotta admit, there've been past complaints about her parting gift of helmet hair."

"No, I meant . . ." Sebastian was listening intently. I had a feeling he knew what I was going to say anyway, so I kept going. "I meant, being here. At Skylark. It's like there's this built-in connection, this way that people have forged me with Jessie Feathering. You must have noticed the way kids look at me but really see her. And considering what happened to her, it's all kind of a lot for me to handle."

"Yeah, sure. I hear that." Sebastian walked me up the porch and dropped into the wicker love seat, pulling me down next to him, and when I swung my legs over so that they bridged his lap, it seemed effortless and natural, a perfect moonlight moment, despite the fact that I was barely awake enough to register it. "And I gotta confess, I listened to the gossip. The Jessie look-alike at Skylark for the summer," he said. "Then when I saw you . . . yeah, I had that moment, too. Like everyone else." He drew a breath. "And there's a void here, with them gone. No doubt of that. There's times it feels like yesterday when I biked to the edge of the bluff to watch the chopper and the rescue boats. Just praying it was all some incredibly bad joke."

Hazily, I conjured it: the helicopter dipping and circling, its propeller rippling into the oppressive heat, the metal sheet of ocean. Sebastian astride his bike at the bluff, sweating and motionless, his eyes trained in disbelief on that same disembodied jut of wing I'd seen on the AP photo that I'd found when I'd looked up the accident online.

I let my hand pause a moment on his scarred forearm. "Sometimes I feel almost guilty about it, like I've unearthed all these bad memories for everyone."

"Jeez, I hope that's not true. 'Cause the reality is the exact opposite. You're a breath of life for Isa. Right before you came into the club, Noogie was telling us all how great you deal with her, how you're already more like a mother to Isa than anyone she's ever had before."

"That's nice, I'm glad to hear that. But this house freaks me out." *Shut up, Jamie.* "It's not at all peaceful; it's restless and angry. It scares me." I clamped my back teeth against my tongue. *Shuttup shuttup.*

"Pete Quint was one of my oldest friends," Sebastian said. "We went to school together from kindergarten. That kid wasn't at peace or very restful when he was alive. I like to think he is now."

I nodded, mute. My head felt like a balloon being jerked by a string.

"Funny thing about Pete, he was really attached to this place," Sebastian continued. "He could have been like one of those Victorian groundskeepers and lived here forever, puttering around and mulching or whatever Victorian groundskeepers did. It was people who made things complicated for him." He let go of this last sentence almost as an afterthought.

"Jessie included?"

"Mostly Jessie included. Or what she represented. A lifetime of lucky breaks. A future on cruise control. She thought Peter was fearless, confident, a winner-take-all type, like her. Which is what he liked her to think."

"Because that's what she wanted?"

"Yeah, and maybe he did, too. Pete's whole family's off-kilter. His old man's basically a hermit. Hasn't spoken twenty words in twenty years."

"And his mom?"

"She ditched them when Pete was a kid," said Sebastian. "She's been living somewhere, I wanna say somewhere outside Boston, for as long as I can remember. Pete used to visit her, and then not so much, when he got older. She never came to Little Bly. She wasn't even at the services last summer."

"Are you kidding?" I snapped a bit more awake at that one. "What kind of mom doesn't go to her son's funeral service?"

"The kind that he had, I guess." Sebastian couldn't disguise that he looked uncomfortable. "Seems morbid, to hash through all this. Anyway." He stretched and shifted, preparing to go. I dropped my legs and stood up with him—if I didn't move in the next minute or so, I'd pass out right here. "You know, Jamie, you might just be coming down with a plain old vanilla summer cold. Try hot water with honey before you crash, and avoid citrus tomorrow. Thousand-year-old theater tricks, but they work."

"Thanks." I walked him down the porch, and back to his bike. Then stepped back as Sebastian turned over the engine.

"Sometimes," I told him, on impulse, "I really do feel that Pete's still here."

"Oh. Okay."

Instantly, I wanted to take it back. Sebastian was embarrassed for me. Which, in a way, was worse than Milo. Milo's contempt made me get defensive. Sebastian's politeness made me feel pathetic.

It was a stupid thing to say. Even if I believed it. Even if it was true. Worse, the one night I'd gotten out and met a guy—a bona fide hottie of a guy, who'd even kissed me, an amazing fireworks of a kiss—I'd ruined everything with my pillhead spooky talk.

Don't say another word Jamie you are way too out of it tonight.

I pressed my lips together, leaned my shoulder against the porch newel. My reserves were almost out.

"Go on . . . I'll watch you in," said Sebastian. "And, Jamie? Don't be scared of the house. I promise, nobody's out to hurt—or even haunt—you." With a small smile. A charity smile?

"Right. G'night," I mumbled, then turned and skimmed up the stairs and through the unlocked door.

I was tired, but not in the right way. Bypassing a toothbrush and a pajama change, I hit into the pillow like an ostrich into sand.

Smoke. Swimming up to consciousness, I knew that it was later. By how much? One hour? Two? My eyes cracked open. The room was black. Silence hung in the air like a spell. My breath tasted rank and my neck hurt, crimped into an unnatural position.

Where was it coming from? Was the house on fire? Fear froze me as Uncle Jim's presence took hold. He was sitting, knees up and crossed like a daddy longlegs, at the foot of my bed. Hank, in the shadows, was in his place, too.

I had to get out and I couldn't. *I don't want to see you anymore I don't want to be you go away leave me alone.* As my body stayed heavy, immobile, I couldn't find my breath, but I needed to move, to leave the room *now now now.*

I snapped back the sheet and jumped like a runner off the block *wee Willie Winkie runs through the town*, down the hall, my breath in thin slices, chasing the steps *upstairs downstairs in his nightgown* to the third floor. The smoke was dense up here. My bare feet pounded as fast as my heart. I ran nearly blind down the hall to the spare room, where *rapping at the windows calling through the locks* I slammed through the door to find a fire blazing, a crackling violence of singeing heat, orange flames bursting up the chimney.

It took another moment to realize they were here, too. On their stomachs, propped by elbows, one leg each hooked at the knee, faces watching the fire *are all the children in their beds for now* as soon as I had opened the door, he turned his head. Through the darkness and the blanket of smoke, his empty stare locked on me, *all the children all the children* and held me tight.

I blinked away to my own reflection on the opposite wall, my shadow rising up like a witch. I jumped and it jumped. I'd gone wet with cold sweat. My eyes caught my shadow and refused to look at him again *because you aren't here, you're in my head and nowhere else.*

"You're not real," I said out loud, much as it petrified me. My voice wasn't mine, but rather a disembodied sound from all around the room. I began backing out the door, my trembling hands like stop signs in front of me; at the last minute, I made the mistake of lifting my gaze to meet his eyes, which were dark and empty as pits.

"You're nothing . . ." my whisper catching sound as we absorbed each other with full knowledge of who the other was, but this wasn't really happening because I was sleepwalking and all I needed to do to end the nightmare was to wake up, *wakeup-wakeup Jamie.* Backing out, stumbling, my mind urging me *wake-upwakeup,* as the edges of my conscious mind went curling, burning up in the fire, and then everything went black.

SIXTEEN

"Jamie."

I opened my eyes. Bright, blue and gold day. Hard shark eyes and hair like frizzed gray rope. Connie was peering down on me. My head throbbed. My neck, my back, ouch. Where was I?

"Look at the time. Look!" She tapped her wristwatch. I blinked. Almost eleven. "I thought you were lollygagging in your room. Then Itha went to check up on you. Thee thaw your bed made up. But I'd heard thome type of motorthycle in the drive latht night. The Brookth boy, I figured."

"Mmm-hmm."

"I looked around the box butheth and hydrangea, in the drive, under the portth . . . thecking if you might not have made it all the way in. But the cat dragged you all the way up here, it theemth. Get up, now. The party ith over. Itha went off with her friend Hannah for the day. Hannah'th mother left you a note. It'th downthtairth."

The slow roll of my livening mind began piecing together that I was on the third floor. Connie must have thought I'd passed out drunk here.

I rolled up, blinking, into a thin patch of sun. I was still in my sundress. Last night flooded back. My eyes darted to the empty hearth, the bed. Which was stacked with blankets and quilts.

Dear Lord. Was *that* what I'd seen? A pile of blankets?

Connie followed my glance. "I'm thorting the winter clo-thet," she said. "Little project I began yethterday. *Get up*."

Faltering onto my feet, crossing the room, I held the wall briefly as the floor swayed and tipped. Connie *tsk*ed. But I had to know. I reached the fireplace and put my hand flat to the hearth. It was cold. "There's fresh ashes in the fireplace."

Connie looked annoyed. "No. I thwept them all when I took out the thquirrel."

"But look." I pointed. "Fresh ashes."

Connie crossed to see. Stooped and traced her finger in the ash. "Itha went through a time when she burned candy wrapperth—getting rid of the evidenth. Lookth like thee might have thneaked back to her old bad habith. It'th only half her fault, in my opinion, what with all that candy they thell over at the Mud Hut. But you thould keep a better eye on her, Jamie—thee'th got a real thweet tooth."

"Right, sure." Everything ached, and I couldn't deal with Connie and her easy explanations right now. I scrambled up and brushed past her, down to my room. I was starving and bleary. The hot shower did some good, and I decided to go cold turkey on the pills today; I wasn't feeling nearly stable enough to risk taking an extra-wrong one, with all of its freaky consequences.

I bypassed the hair dryer to get breakfast: two full bowls of cereal plus the fruit smoothie that Connie had placed in the fridge. I stepped out onto the porch to drink it.

The light of day made order of last night's chaos.

What had I done? *Okay, run through it, Jamie.* I'd taken a sleeping pill. I'd mixed it with a tiny bit of alcohol. I'd hallucinated and become disoriented. I'd told Sebastian a lot of loony, wild stuff—but I could have told him worse, and I didn't. Then I'd gone to sleep and I'd had a nightmare, which caused me to go wandering around the house in a semi-sleepwalking fit of temporary madness in which I'd seen what I thought was Jessie and Peter, but which had turned out to be a stack of laundry.

As for those ashes, Isa easily could have burned some candy wrappers. I'd had to monitor some of her candy-buying sprees at the Mud Hut before; it was a perfectly reasonable explanation.

Milo was on the front lawn, bare-chested and juggling an assortment of objects. I knew where he'd gotten them. They usually lived on a silver bar trolley in the parlor.

A letter opener, a china dog, and a glass paperweight. Milo's movements were supple and assured.

"I'll hand it to you," I admitted. "You're not bad."

"Pete taught me last summer." As the knickknacks spun weightless. "Pete taught me everything. Everything I am, I owe him. To the point where sometimes I feel like I *am* him." He smirked. "Come to think of it, maybe I inherited his soul."

My heart raced. "Don't say that. Don't even joke. I thought we'd buried the hatchet on all that stuff."

"Too late. Everything is officially unburied, Jamie. You of all people should know that." One by one, Milo caught them; dog, paperweight, letter opener, all safe, and then he bowed. "You look like death served cold," he remarked. "Is that how Jersey Girls like to wear their hair?"

"Really, Milo?" I swallowed. "That's the best you can do?"

His gaze flicked off me. He stuck the objects in his pockets, pivoted and then began a series of studied hand movements that looked like martial arts; it reminded me of Teddy's brief junior-year romance with tae kwon do. "Your negativity is sucking the *chi* out of the atmosphere," he informed. "Stop watching me."

I did. Back in the kitchen, I found the note from Hannah Smart's mom, explaining that she'd picked up Isa to pal along with Hannah, who was enrolled in some crafts workshop in town. "We'll be back later in the afternoon, probably close to three o'clock."

I crunched the note into the trash. So now the whole island's worth of moms would be buzzing like bumblebees that the McRae au pair was so irresponsible that she partied all night and slept all morning.

Ah, yes. That was just great.

Alone, with the whole day on my hands and too many details of last night like a packed jack-in-the-box that I wasn't quite ready to pop out, I stole into the den. Miles's computer was there, and I checked Facebook to retrieve mail from Mags, Tess and Teddy.

When I typed SEBASTIAN BROOKS, I got a cute if ridiculous profile picture of Sebastian from a few years back, dressed as the

Scarecrow from *The Wizard of Oz*, and I laughed out loud. Must have been a school play. This guy had no fear. There was the standard message that I had to be friends with Sebastian Brooks before he shared any information. To request his friendship at this stage was way too eagersville; I got off, and then, on impulse, I typed SEAN RYAN.

Although there was a seemingly endless supply of Sean Ryans in the data bank, I found his profile picture so quick, it slapped me back. But there he was. Exactly the same but changed, reinvented in a photograph of himself as Mr. Outdoorsman. Straddling a bicycle, his face obscured by aviators, with a cliché view of the mountains behind him.

Sean Ryan, Mr. Colorado. Desperate for people to think he was awesome. Mr. Chemistry Nerd, Mr. Mellow Teacher, Mr. Helpful Guy.

Mr. Hit the Refresh Button, after his Mr. Mistake Year.

In the search bar, I typed the name JESSIE FEATHERING. That profile was invalid, of course. The Featherings sounded like the type of people who'd have kept tabs on all those final arrangements and small considerations, like disconnecting a Facebook profile.

As I searched PETER QUINT, something in me was sure that his page would be open.

I was right. I dragged my pointer slow and careful as a hand along the tiny postage stamp of Peter's profile picture. His eyes looked translucent. But I knew him already, of course, even as his actual photo unnerved me. He was the kid from the cliffs. He was Jessie's sketch. The boy in the rain, through the window and on the bed.

And he knows you see him, Jamie, the way he stared at you last night but don't think about that because you didn't see him it was a sleeping pill it was a night terror.

I slid the cursor to the toolbar to exit the program. I clicked, and the drop-down menu showed me the previous user: PDQUINT.

My fingers snapped off the keys. Shock. Breathe. The last person to log on to Facebook before me, from this computer, was Peter. I steadied my breath. Okay, but that made sense. Milo and Isa preferred the family-room computer. Connie never used one. And Miles McRae hadn't touched it, as evidenced by the fact that there were no marked tabs or bookmarks, no downloads. It was only for show—like his cigar humidor and scotch decanters and that spinning globe—to complete his gentleman's den.

I double-clicked on Pete's name.

PASSWORD?

Imagine, if I knew that password, then I'd be inside, with access to all Pete's private notes and comments and images. It was a Pandora's box. I had no other choice—or hardly any—than to try.

I typed in SKYLARK, and it shot me back an INCORRECT.

Next, I typed JESSIE. Denied.

All variations of JESSIE and PETER, of FEATHERING and QUINT, even of MILO and ISA MCRAE. Nothing, nothing.

"Just as well," I muttered. Nights were bad enough; why fill my days with phantoms, too? Even if I wanted to research Peter Quint's data bank, his friends and messages and photos, what did I need to get to the bottom of, anyway? What did I need to expose?

Nothing you need nothing so leave it alone you don't need any of this.

I shut down. My head hurt, my back hurt. I needed a pill. I

needed all the pills. My mind shuffled rapid-fire images—bottomless eyes, Sean Ryan on his trendy mountain bike in front of his trendy mountain range, Milo's smirk as the letter opener spun up through the air like a knife *everything is officially unburied, Jamie.*

All of it was chewing, chewing at my brain like that frantic, trapped squirrel unable to *bong, bong, bong.*

The grandfather clock in the hall was striking the half hour *the mouse ran down hickory-dickory* while at the same time the doorbell had been ringing *brring, brring.* All these bells, but the door was probably just Mrs. Smart, back and curious for a quick check to see if all my lazy bones were present and accounted for.

I logged off, then ran out of the den to answer the door.

"Oh." I stepped back. "You."

"Me." Sebastian touched his forehead in a two-fingered salute. "It's my lunch hour, so I thought I'd come by to check on your fake hangover. Plus I wanted to ask you out to Rocco's. It's on the harbor. Best lunch in town. They practically catch the fish with the griddle pan."

I hesitated, one hand working subtly to smooth down my hair. My adrenaline was sloshing from the surprise of seeing him. Should I go? Or should I be here, in case Isa returned before three?

"Say yes." He looked so fresh and crisp, his hair like tarnished gold bristles.

"I didn't think I'd be meeting up with you again, after what a mess I was last night."

"Maybe I'm a sucker for your drama. And you sure bring it." Squinting slightly, with his thumbs stuck in his belt loops, and his sunny, extravagant smile tuned in to me alone, Sebastian made last night seem funny, like nothing. And if this guy was willing to give me a break on last night, I'd be glad to give myself a break, too.

And then, to my dismay, Milo. He'd located a T-shirt and shoes, and raced up from behind to stand on the bottom tread of the porch steps. "Oooh, Jamie's got a boyfriend."

I refocused on Sebastian's eyes—a speckled amber, by the light of day—while studiously ignoring Milo. And those ears, had I noticed Sebastian's exceptionally cute ears last night? Because they were adorable, tipping out just slightly on the ends so that the sun glinted through the cartilage, giving him a sweetly ethereal, star-boy quality.

"Listen, I need a ride over to Stonyfield." Milo took the remaining couple of steps so that we were all at level gaze. He stood with arms crossed, and I knew he was flexing his biceps. It was almost sweet if I hadn't been so annoyed. "I got selected to play in the junior golf tournament, and, uh, I wanted to get some practice in. Gimme a lift?"

Sebastian just raised his eyebrows. He didn't want to, I could tell. He wouldn't even break eye contact with me. Was still waiting for my answer, which said it all. Milo could try all he wanted, but he was just a kid. And a pest—who was best left ignored, as Emory had put it.

"Speak now or I'm taking that as a yes," said Milo, whining slightly, but undeterred. "So we'll go in Dad's car?"

There was no arguing it. Milo was a real force, not the type to go quietly now that he was here, especially if he sensed resistance. And Sebastian was waiting for me to decide what to do.

"Take it as a yes," I said to Milo.

Then, to Sebastian, "We'll borrow Miles's car. Let me get the keys, plus my flops. Okay by you?"

"Aw, chicken. You're just scared of Bonnie's four-speed horsepower," he teased. "But yeah, that's fine by me."

"Two seconds," I said, returning his smile, which seemed almost dangerously contagious. "Be right back."

SEVENTEEN

Officially, Milo's niggling presence was not going to bother me. He could smirk and undermine and be disdainful all he wanted, but I'd resolved to keep my cool and hold my own.

"Big Rocco's the man," Sebastian mentioned as we parked, then walked to the wharf. He had a loose but directed stride that was easy for me to fall in step with. "There, that's him." As a stout guy came barreling out of the restaurant, a wagon-wheel-sized tray balanced over his shoulder.

"*Big* Rocco." I grinned. Rocco couldn't have been more than five feet. The place was the definition of a local secret, a corrugated tin shed right on the harbor, with lunches arriving in red-checked paper boats.

Milo hadn't mentioned any turnoff to Stonyfield, and Sebastian didn't even bother to ask him. Which only confirmed my suspicion that his golf date had been a complete ruse. Milo was sticking with us, tagging along and waiting for me to act gauche or say something Jersey Girl. The kid brother I never wanted. Well, he could bring it on. I was too wrapped up in Sebastian, and my second chance with him, to care.

The view was pretty, a colorful homecoming of tied sailboats and schooners with a couple of yachts bobbing farther out in the harbor. I inhaled ocean air, brine and browned butter. The noon-day sun and the pitcher of lemon ice water that arrived when we sat drenched the moment in summertime bliss that made it seem immediately nostalgic.

Sebastian turned up his face to the sky and closed his eyes. "I'm going for my standard—a batter-fried clam sandwich."

"I think I'll have that, too," I said.

Milo made a barf noise, then slumped in his seat. "She orders what he orders. Way to show your hand. I've lost my appetite to you lovebirds. Looks like you've fallen pretty hard, Jamie. So now I know that even Jersey Girls with gold plastic sandals get soul mates. Who'da thought?"

I reddened, glad for Sebastian's gentlemanly disregard of what turned out to be Milo's last dig. He lapsed into near-total silence, letting Sebastian lead the talk in easy hops from bands he liked to plays he'd seen to the ideal summer job.

"How's yours?" I asked.

"It's intense. Running a laundry can be an obstacle course," Sebastian explained. "Lifting, sorting, folding, ironing. See these scars?" He rubbed his finger along the marks. "My war wounds. Years of run-ins with the steam iron."

"Ouch." I winced. While inwardly, I guess I sank a little. Not self-inflicted, after all. Was I disappointed? Had Sebastian's scars made him more accessible? I hated to think it, but they probably did.

On the drive home, Sebastian directed me to a gas station. It was off Bush, along a one-way road, cupped with potholes and crumbled to gravel on its edges, and was lined with modest cottages, their land tracts divided by fences or chicken wire.

"Most of what you've seen on Bly is theater. This is backstage," said Sebastian. "Laurel Lane is also known as Local's Lane, Yokel Lane . . . it's almost one hundred percent year-rounders. My folks and I live a mile down. But right there, that's Augie Quint's place."

The house next to the gas station was hardly more than a paint-chipped shed, though the twin pots of geraniums on the stoop added a painstaking measure of dignity. The thought preoccupied me as we got gas and drove home, the wind clean on my skin, my body warmed just right between the car's expensive leather and the canopy of sun and trees. Wondering what it had been like for Peter to grow up with that brooding parent, in that humble house, with all this wealth, this summertime paradise all around him.

Back at Skylark, Milo finally got bored with playing the third wheel and vanished around back. Sebastian and I were left alone on the porch. "I should shove off soon—there was a post-regatta bash over at the club last night. Heard it turned pretty wild toward the early hours. So today'll be nothing but red-wine stains and gossip about who had a few too many and who made a pass at whose wife." Sebastian rolled his eyes but made no attempt to shove off; instead, he sank into the swing chair, rocking himself back and forth with the ball of one foot.

"I'm not sure I really get Little Bly," I said.

"What's to get? A town this small isn't exactly complicated."

"No, but there's an intimacy to it. How everyone's got information on everyone else. How you literally know their dirty laundry. Look, I'm not knocking it—this island is beautiful. But it's not a place I'd want to live for keeps, with people whispering about where I was last night and who I might have been hitting on and how I stained my shirt. No offence."

"No problem." Sebastian leaned over and jabbed a finger lightly between my ribs. "None taken."

I poked him back. He yelped and twisted away. "Aha!" I crowed, moving in to get him harder. "And now I know that you are ticklish."

"Oh, game *on*, babe." But not really; or, rather, a game that quickly turned into something entirely different as Sebastian pulled me down on his lap, and the poking and pinching ceased as his mouth found mine. "See, this is the sweet part about being in the family business," he said softly. "'Cause the family understands when you tell 'em you need to leave work on account of a cute girl."

"Is there an un-sweet part?"

"Yep." That flash of smile.

"Which is?"

"Ducking the thousand questions that my family'll interrogate me with after."

"So you think I'm cute?"

Sebastian made a show of considering this question. "Submitted physical evidence indicates that, *oui, mademoiselle*. You are cute. No debate."

It was a moment when he might have worked in another

kiss, though he didn't take it. Skylark didn't feel like the most private atmosphere anyway, what with Connie's presence like a creeping mold, dampening from the sidelines.

Minutes later, walking back to his bike, Sebastian opened the seat, where he flipped me a tattered paperback. "When does Isa roll home?"

I checked the cover—*Romeo and Juliet*. I glanced at my watch. "She's not due back for another hour. But if that's for her, she'll be psyched. *Romeo and Juliet*'s her favorite movie, she told me."

"Her favorite movie was Pete's favorite play," Sebastian explained. "Our high school put it on this past spring to honor his memory. I was Romeo, and I used Pete's own script with his notes from junior-year English lit. It was a strange kind of access, being inside his mind. Intense. Anyway." He shook off the chill of the thought.

"I'd have liked to see you in your cute little Romeo tights."

"Sorry, blue jeans. We staged it like *West Side Story*. School budget restrictions." He was talking about one thing, but his index finger was moving up and down my arm. I shivered.

"I'd have liked to see the blue-jeans version, too," I said.

"Well, I wish I'da known you then."

"I'll be sure that she gets this." I riffled the pages. Peter's spiky handwriting leaped out at me.

Sebastian straddled the cycle seat and pulled on his old-fashioned helmet, buckling the padded strap. "Hey, I almost forgot. There's this kick-ass band, Eight Feet Deep, and they've actually made a date to play at Little Bly, which pretty much never happens. Not this Saturday, but next, and it's on Finley

131

Beach. I'd guess ninety percent of the island's going, or at least the music-loving percent. You want to come, too? With me, I mean?"

"Okay." A date. With Sebastian. *Yes yes yes.*

"I'll pick you up here at eight."

I got bold. "That's days and days away," I said.

He looked embarrassed. "Way too planned, Brooks. Way, way, too, too."

"No," I laughed. "It's not that. It's just, I mean—you can come by here anytime before. You know, if you want."

"Yeah, okay. Sounds good. You've got the best pool."

"Well, come for the pool, then."

"I didn't mean it like that, I mean, obviously, there are better incentives. Okay, you know what? I'm gonna stop talking." Then he took the moment, and the kiss. Definitely leading-man material. He smelled perfect, like starch and sunshine. As soon as the kiss was over I wanted another, identical one. And another, and another, like a bunch of sweet grapes. Whatever else this summer had been or might become, I'd met Sebastian—and there was nobody here, or back home, whose kisses I'd craved more.

I watched him take off down the drive before I went around back, to Connie's kitchen garden. She'd turned on the sprinklers. Thyme, basil, mint, flat parsley . . . I inhaled the wet warmth of fragrance. I dropped to lie down on my stomach in the grass, then propped up on my elbows to open the play. Light and leaves cast its pages in a lacy pattern.

Languid and heat-warmed, I drifted into Verona, the warring Capulets and Montagues, the dense language of another era . . . this no-pill day was turning out to be no problem after all . . . I dozed. . . .

"You look like an angel when you sleep."

I twisted and sat up, too fast. Pain nailed blunt rivets up my spine.

"Sorry." Aidan McNabb was kneeling over me, his face blocking my sun. "Didn't mean to startle you."

"How'd you get here?" I scrabbled back, creating some space between us since Aidan was, as usual, a touch too close. "I didn't hear a car."

"I walked. My landscape job's right there." As he pointed inland.

"The Grosvenor place."

"Right." Without my asking, he reached for my hand and pulled me up. Aidan was a lot of person, more beefy than strong; even his hand was well fed and round as a mitt. *Aidan Aidan, pudding and pie, kissed the girls and made them cry.*

"Was that Sibby Brooks's putt-putt I heard a few minutes ago?"

"Uh-huh."

"Guess he beat me to it."

"To what?"

"Checking up on you. You seemed kinda out of it last night." As Aidan shook his head, his gaze was unnerving; it seemed to lick me up and down like a tongue. "It's unreal. You could be her sister."

"So is this checking up on me, or checking me out?"

"Ha, yeah, good one." Aidan was wearing crisp khaki work shorts and a spotless nectarine-orange polo. I could see the recent track of comb marks in Aidan's hair; the thought of him combing and preening before he set off to find me gave me a tiny shudder. He sure didn't appear worried about being away from

133

work, and he didn't look like he'd done much heavy lifting for old Mrs. Grosvenor today, either. I started walking toward the house. I didn't exactly love being cloistered in the back garden with this guy.

"Wait up," he said. "What's the rush? You in a hurry to get somewhere?"

I turned. Aidan's hazel eyes were warm, almost girlishly pretty, with long curling eyelashes. But the greedy way he kept staring at me negated anything attractive about his eyes. "I'm just waiting for Isa is all." I glanced at the kitchen door and hoped Connie wasn't witnessing any of this—Sebastian at lunch, Aidan in the afternoon: yeesh.

Aidan was standing too close again. "You coming out next Saturday? Finley Beach? I could pick you up."

"Actually, I'm going with Sebastian."

"Uh-oh. I was afraid of that."

"What do you mean?"

A smile thinned his lips. "You should know Brooks has got a college girlfriend. And, word of advice, you might not want to get too exclusive with the local talent."

I gave him a look. "What's that mean?"

"Look, Sebastian's way chill. We hang. But Jessie got wrapped up in her own local, and we all know how that ended."

It was a harsh thing to say, but in Aidan's face I also could read something different, more deeply buried and maybe even more tender than he was used to admitting. "You were close with Jessie," I said. It was why he was here, of course. He was looking for her, in me. "You miss her."

He'd gone tense, as if trying to assess what I knew. Whether I was bluffing, maybe. "Sure. She was a great girl."

134

"Really close, I meant. Or maybe it was that you wanted to be close. Am I right?"

"Why would you . . . I . . ." There was an almost audible slamming up of Aidan's defenses, but before he could speak, I caught a movement on the other side of the hedgerow.

"Hello?" I pivoted. "Who's there?"

There wasn't any way to get around the hedgerow. I sprinted for the driveway.

"There's no one," Aidan called from behind me. "I've got twenty-twenty. I can practically see through walls."

I was convinced I'd detected something. One of the gardeners? Pool guys? People showed up at Skylark all day to mow, weed, water, prune and filter. "Hello?" I repeated, my ears pricked, my body poised to pursue one direction or another.

In answer, the rustle of a warm wind in the trees.

The butt of the cigarette was pinched. I leaned down and picked it off the flagstone. It was cold and stale, discarded months ago.

Then I saw it, scraped hard into the slate: **J + P 8/16**

The day they died. My heart was slamming around like a racquetball against my ribs. Who'd done this? When? *As if you didn't know. The J looks exactly the same, a perfect match to the third floor.*

Aidan was on my heel. "Was it anyone?"

Using my foot, I quickly pushed over a couple of stray magnolia leaves to conceal the letters. "Nobody," I told him. "False alarm. And seriously, Aidan. I think you'd better go. Now that you've seen me up close in the light of day, you can tell beyond all doubt that I'm not Jessie, right?"

"It wasn't about . . ." His roundly handsome face looked

baffled, then just plain annoyed. "Guess I can't compete with the laundry boy," he said, thrusting his hands into his pockets and, thankfully, backing off for the first time.

"Oh, don't worry. It was never a competition," I told him, keeping my tone bright. "And last I checked, you were officially seeing someone else."

"It's what you're doing unofficially that makes life interesting," Aidan quipped lightly. Still, in some bizarre way, trying to charm me.

"I'm sure Emory would be fascinated to hear that," I said. Not lightly.

His eyes narrowed. I held my ground and my gaze. After all, he'd started it. No matter who he wished I were or what he wanted me to be. But I was relieved when Aidan finally gave up on me and left.

EIGHTEEN

"Who was your last boyfriend?"

Isa and Connie had gone up to bed hours ago. But Milo and I had stayed down in the family room, watching a spy thriller now gone to commercial.

The smack of his question had me on immediate guard. "Why're you asking?"

Milo's face was sly. "Just, if you're into Sebastian Brooks these days, I hope you've had some experience. Sibby isn't gonna like a tease."

In answer, my yawn. But I was a coiled spring.

Until this moment, we'd had a good night. Surprisingly. I'd let go of my paranoia about Milo, that he was testing and undermining me. I wanted to make the effort for Isa, who'd noticed the change enough to comment on it.

"Good, you're talking to Miley again," she'd said. "Everyone's friends." Though I could tell that Connie was less enthused, since any of our allegiances tended to shut her out. But it had been an easy evening, as we'd all helped Connie prepare a pasta-salad dinner, followed by fresh rhubarb cobbler, and then even indulged in a few of Isa's disorganized, boring rounds of twenty questions.

But now Milo was at it again. Expertly jabbing at the place where I was most vulnerable. "You think a guy like Brooks only wants to hold hands with you, you're on the wrong side of wrong."

"Why don't you let me worry about that?"

Lazily, he began cherry-picking objects—a plastic cup, his wallet, and one of Isa's sandals—to juggle. I watched them spin, seemingly lost to the laws of gravity. Juggling also kept Milo from having to look me in the eye directly as he continued talking. "I've got private intel about that guy. Insider stuff, the kinds of things an outsider like you wouldn't have a clue about."

"Uh-huh, sure." But I was listening. Waiting for it.

"Like, for example, he's totally gone on this college girl. Some blonde. I remember last year how she'd come down—"

"You know what, Milo? You've got a big ole yap. And it's gotten you in trouble in the past, right? So, before you say anything markedly stupid, think about it."

"Hey, I'm only trying to protect you. It's not my fault you're working that sulk."

"What sulk?"

"That sulk of a chick who's been burned. Who was it—some football tool who threw you over for a cuter pair of pom-poms? Or a sensitive hipster boy? Or maybe your teacher. You can tell me. How'd he break your heart?"

"Word of advice—don't become a private investigator, Milo. You'll go out of business in a month." Though once again, I was in a pure reaction state as Milo worked his uncanny ability to whittle me down to my weakest self.

"Look, I'm only warning you, Bass has seen some lovin', no doubt—hey!" As my foot, acting almost with a mind of its own, suddenly kicked up and sideswiped him, buckling his knee, throwing him off balance. The plastic cup fell out; he tried to catch it back and couldn't. Cursing, he dropped back on the couch, nearly on top of me.

"What's your problem?" As I scooted out from under him, Milo jettisoned himself forward, smoothly pushing up and over my body and pinning me into the couch cushions.

My hands pummeled him. "Get off me, you loser. I'm not in the mood to deal with any of this."

"Who's the loser? I'd be doing you a favor. And you should get in some practice. He'll smell that inexperience on you." I could feel the warmth radiating from Milo's skin as his hand smoothed my hair from my face. "If it's not me, your next best bet is up in your bedroom, making out with your pillow, am I right?"

I shoved him with my feet, hard, then sat up, breathing out my anger in bursts. "Thanks but no thanks. I think I'll be just fine without your tutorial."

The next moment was silence. I waited for him to go first.

"You might need it more than you think."

I went rigid. Milo's voice wasn't his own anymore. It was low, an entirely different cadence and octave. But I couldn't look at him, I couldn't even speak. I waited. "After all, we both know you're the crazy one, Jamie."

"I'm not crazy," I whispered. "Stop talking like that."

"You're onto what happened here," he continued in the same hollowed tone that didn't belong to Milo at all. "How it all went down. They say that the crazy people can always see clear down to the ugliest truth. Problem is, nobody believes 'em. But all you need's a little proof, right?"

"Stop it." When I forced myself to glance over, Milo looked exactly the same. It was his expression—his daredevil smirk—that belonged to someone else. "Seriously, stop it, Milo. I know what you're doing."

"Oh, really? What am I doing?"

"You know what, it's like you're imitating him, you're allowing him, somehow, you're letting him into the space—*stop it!*" That smirk! I couldn't restrain myself; I lunged, my fingertips like pincers digging at Milo's skin, yanking at his shoulders, his neck like dough *roll it and prick it and mark it and prick it and mark it* as Milo yelped and leaped panther-like out of my grasp, jumping to perch on the armrest on the opposite end of the couch. I was breathing hard; my entire body was shaking with panic.

Get control of yourself, Jamie. Nothing good happens when you lose control of yourself.

I pressed my hands to my blazing cheeks.

"Jeez, Jamie. Way to take a joke."

"You weren't . . ." What had come over me? I'd gone and attacked this kid . . . he could call his father and report me . . . worse. "I'm s-sorry," I stammered. "I'm not . . . not sure what came over me. For a minute I thought you'd become—that you'd turned—"

"Turned what?" he demanded. Glaring and scornful.

Turned into Peter. But I couldn't force myself to say it out loud. "I don't know. I don't know what else to say. You scared me. You shouldn't have talked in that voice. It wasn't funny. I'm not crazy, but I am sorry."

He dropped to the seat, exaggeratedly wary, as if I were some attack dog now chained. "Fine. Then I'm sorry, too."

"Let's just forget it, then."

"Sure. Whatever. Already forgotten." Only his tone told me otherwise as he stood. "I'm going up now. I'm beat."

But by now I was collecting my thoughts and my reason. This hadn't been entirely my fault. Milo didn't see me as all the way "normal" and he took advantage of it, throwing his voice, freaking me out with his singular, menacing ability to channel Peter. This was all an intentional, elaborate invention for Milo, an amateur magician's game to frighten and destabilize me. Then, as soon as I lost it, all he had to do was pull back and claim innocence.

Uneasily, I picked up the empty dessert plates, and Milo clicked off the television.

We moved clumsily through the next few minutes, excessively polite to each other as we headed upstairs, where I rinsed the dishes and wiped down the counters. But Milo had gone so quiet that new thoughts collided through me. What if Peter actually *had* manifested himself through Milo? What if I'd witnessed something, some kind of split-second transmutation, that even Milo himself wasn't fully aware of?

Milo wasn't talking. His silence seemed impenetrable, so I didn't make an attempt at false conversation. We said goodnights and he left. I was still nervously over-tidying the kitchen when Isa came stumbling in, red-eyed and whining sleepily.

"I went down to your room and you weren't there. I had

another nightmare, that I was falling through the sky and I couldn't—what's wrong?" Suddenly she was right up in my face. I blinked. "Jamie, are you in one of your trances again?"

"My trances?"

"Sometimes you go away. You're here but you're not here."

"Very funny." Except I knew all too well what she meant. How, I wondered stupidly, in the thousandth iteration of this thought, would I ever get off these pills? They were making me see things, they'd turned Milo into Peter, but every time another one wore off, all I could think about was getting the next. It would require some act of extreme will or meditation or—

"LIKE RIGHT NOW!" Isa's hand was flapping in front of my face. "There's times like right now," she repeated, more gently, "when I'll be talking to you, and I know you haven't heard what I just said."

Good Lord, what was my problem? *Focus, focus.* "What did you just say?"

"I asked if you'd make me a milk and honey."

"Sure." Capably, my au pair persona re-pinned like a nurse's hat, I took out a saucepan for the milk. After Isa drank it, I took her upstairs to her bedroom. Although I didn't want to, I couldn't leave without checking the fireplace.

More tiles had been chipped out. A few lay broken in the grate. Shivering, I rushed from the room and sped down the hall, nearly tripping over myself, my eyes averted from the portrait of the ghostly children, my hand out to grab the doorknob, not stopping until I'd locked myself safe in my own room.

Where I was too jittery to sleep. I tried a hot shower, my fuzzy socks, the radio tuned softly to classical, and then flipping through my journal, which was an absolute mess. I'd hardly been marking the dates and my thoughts seemed haphazard. My *Mother Goose's Nursery Rhymes* was in my top bureau drawer; for the first time, I took it out and flipped through its pages. The illustrations—round-cheeked children in pinafores, with their flower garlands and quaint toys—always used to soothe me, but tonight the words seemed extra ominous. *Pop*—had the weasel exploded? And what had possessed Dumpty, a man made from raw egg, to scale a wall? The three blind mice reminded me of the portrait children outside my door.

With a shiver, I closed the book and shoved it into the nightstand.

Eventually, I picked up *Romeo and Juliet*. Peter's spidery, over-slanted handwriting marked the play with notes like "joy before death?" "no way out but violence, passion, death." It was pretty clear that Peter saw himself as a dark Romeo, the reckless romantic.

Midway through the second act, I butterflied the play and crept out of bed to the bookcase. Giving in. Justifying it. My back was still throbbing from the jolt my tailbone had taken, riding on the back of Sebastian's bike last night.

So what if I needed something? It was just an itty-bitty little something.

I had a good handful of pills left. And then what? Did Connie have a stash? Would over-the-counters work? I couldn't think that far ahead. I popped one, praying that it was just your basic painkiller.

Crawling to bed, I returned to Peter's notes in the play, pausing to read the back inside cover.

We live with minimal awareness of why we choose
certain paths. We are predetermined but we can't
escape ourselves—our families—our characters—
our destiny.

It was a bleak vision, especially as I applied it to myself. What if Uncle Jim's and Hank's choices weren't choices at all? What if they were destined from birth to meet their troubled ends? Did they know my future, my fate, before I did? Was that why they persisted? Would they hunt me down at my most vulnerable moment, the moment before The Moment, forever?

An ornately gilt-framed oil painting hung above the fireplace. I stared at it as I had nearly every night before. A European city street at twilight. Narrow buildings hunkered over the cobblestone. Red flowers on the balcony splashed its only spot of color. I imagined Juliet standing there, delirious with longing and wishing that her beloved wasn't

The word switched on like the click of a flashlight.

Moments later, swift on my toes, my mouth pressed tense every time the floorboards gave, I found my way into Miles McRae's darkened den, where I turned on the computer and logged in as PQUINT.

PASSWORD?

MONTAGUE.

And then, like a key to the treasure room, Peter Quint's home page opened.

He'd died almost a year ago, but here on his Facebook, he continued to exist in cyberheaven, still visited by loved ones who had plastered his wall with photographs of lilies and wreaths, and notes and passages from the Bible. I skimmed them all, and then clicked into his stash of private messages, over two hundred of them unread. Probably more tributes, so I didn't bother to read them, but instead scrolled all the way back to the oldest messages, the read messages, from when Peter was alive.

Here was one from Sebastian, referring to an incident where Pete had let his temper get the best of him. Sebastian's note was characteristically forgiving and teasing: u CANT be the guy in the bar with the gut throwing punches and busting walls cuz dude we all know that guy and he sux.

Another friend, Greg Doonan, had sent notes on fishing conditions off the Sound. Another guy sent photos of his dog pretending to drink beer. I didn't know any of these kids. They were Pete's school friends, his fishing buddies. I began to pick up the messages from Jessie, though there was never anything particularly revealing from her, either. She'd been as caught up as anybody in the day-to-day of life on Bly, though I did sense her daring in the messages, especially the fascination with flying in her father's prop plane—which, in one message, Jessie had described to Peter as better than sex, am I rite? jk! kinda!

Of course it was wrong of me to read them. No matter that he had died, I was still intruding in on Peter's private memories, and his most intimate relationship. My entire body was taut with the transgression, the strange dip-diving fear, absorbing all of this information that didn't belong to me.

Staring at the albums, I could hear the stick in my own breath, feel the chalky swallow after I'd forgotten to swallow. Jessie loved the camera, she vamped and pouted for it. Her figure was curvier, her hair wilder, her features more lush and ripe than mine. In one picture, she was showing off her silver tongue piercing; in another, I caught a glimpse of a blue butterfly tattoo at her hip bone. But now I could see the resemblance, through the prism of all her angles and expressions. Jessie Feathering looked more like me than my own sister—except that I was the diminished version, the ghost of her.

I clicked open Pete's last read message, from Jessie, that had been sent the day before the accident.

```
Way to be a jerk not showing at
green hill today. I'm pretty sure we
had plans, y? What is it about
Pendleton that makes you come back
from there being such a tubocharge
jackass? gets boring, Chippy & i
don't know what you think you know,
or what Isa told you, but take it
with a grain of salt. Isa can be
freakishly imaginative.
    And as for what She told you—
that's such a joke I wont even
dignify it with a defense.
    P: I luv you & I think we're
great together. But not when ur in a
mood, not when ur an insecure
paranoid. If you want me in ur life,
then roll with my choices. What's
left to say? Drop me a line if you
feel like it.
```

I sat there utterly still in the darkness and frowned into the puzzle of the text.

What had Isa said? *Pendleton*, where was that? *She*, who was She?

Too many questions and nowhere to find answers. I opened a new window, typed in a search and got parks, towns, shops and even a racetrack named Pendleton.

When I typed in JESSIE FEATHERING, I found the same old AP news brief all about the crash, plus some local coverage of the funerals, and then a tribute site that had been set up at Jessie's school. A local link went to a photo, a sweetly smiling Jessie, younger than I'd ever seen her, and names—Jessie was the daughter of Patricia and John, Peter was the son of August and Katherine—but I knew most of these details already, from previous searching.

I returned to Jessie's message. In my original picture of Peter and Jessie, they'd been two star-crossed opposites whose relationship had stirred the conflict between Bly's lifers and locals. What everyone had seemed to agree on, however, was that the two of them were deeply in love with each other. Or (at the very least) deeply infatuated.

And yet this offhand, prickly, irritated note, written by Jessie only the day before they died, didn't fit the picture of soul mates. This note spelled trouble between them.

NINETEEN

"I'm biking into town to pick up a prescription at the pharmacy," I said. "Back in an hour or so. I'll have my cell."

Connie and Isa nodded. They were in round six of a Crazy Eights–athon. "And you'll need to pick up a can of thtainleth thteel thcrubber," said Connie, who never liked me to go anywhere without carting back a domestic offering.

Not a question = no answer. Please. *Get your own scrubber, Funsicle.*

Miles's Trek bike was in the garage. Why hadn't I thought to use it before? Before I'd thrown my back, I'd always relied on a long run to unwind whatever pressure had wrung knots in my day. Sweat off my problems, exhaust my mind as I burned out my body. A bike might be easier on me, physically—only how long since I'd taken out a bicycle?

Once upon a time, bikes were Mags and my main escape route: to the movies or Friendly's or cutting across the highway to Walgreens, where we wasted hours in the Crafts aisle, pondering the purchase of stuff we didn't need. But those days got junked with our Schwinns the second we passed our driving tests.

Hitting the open road was an old joy. I'd set a bad precedent that first morning, using Miles's sports car. Isa didn't like riding her bike—outside of diving class, she was a bit of a house cat, and she definitely saw riding in her dad's awesome convertible as the height of summertime chic.

Maybe getting her onto a bike, motivating us both into some kind of daily exercise routine, would be my next au pair project. We could use it.

Bush Road was serene, with a hush of wind in the grasses tossed wild along its borders. Hardly any cars passed me on my way. It wasn't until I wheeled through the wrought-iron gate and leaned the bike against a massive oak that I felt a tug of anxiety. I'd found the address in the Bly directory, but I hadn't called ahead. At the time, it had seemed too formal a thing to do.

Now I wasn't sure.

Like so many of the island's residences, 58 Shoal was imposing—a starchy Victorian with bay windows, protected by a stately gathering of beeches and silver lindens. I wanted to turn back. But I kept on going, hands balled in my shorts pockets, force-marching myself right up to the front door.

It had been nearly a week since I'd found Pete's Facebook. I'd tried to forget about it. I'd focused on Isa. Yesterday, I'd broken the routine of the beach and pool by taking her out shopping in Little Bly's tiny, arty center of town. Isa always blossomed under my full attention, which made me happy—especially since it also meant I'd hardly had to interact with Milo at all.

But then last night, I found myself wide awake and restless and, eventually, floating online again. Mulling over that last direct message from Jessie. So many secrets seemed to be encoded inside—like the references to Peter's not showing up at the beach, her halfhearted defense against Isa's story, and Pendleton and that maddeningly mysterious *She*. Plus there were other thistly details: Jessie's using the word *luv* instead of *love*, the off-hand assurance that she and Pete were "great together" when he wasn't "an insecure paranoid" and the casual command that he should roll with her choices.

What choices? What was Jessie really saying here?

Also, the message wasn't signed with Jessie's usual *x*'s and *o*'s.

Finally, while she was clearly irritated with Pete for bailing on their plan to meet up at Green Hill, Jessie made no references to plans for the next day. Almost as if she couldn't care less what he was up to. All in all, not very girlfriendy.

Or maybe I'd overanalyzed it. It wouldn't be the first time I'd read too much into something.

A uniformed housekeeper answered on my first press of the bell.

"Hi." I cleared the shyness from my throat. "I'm looking for Emory? I work over at Skylark. For the McRae family?" My own name seemed irrelevant.

"Emory's here, but she's napping," said the housekeeper, with a very Connie-ish lilt of disdain in her voice.

"Oh." I raised my eyebrows and drew up my lips in a reaction of mild astonishment, an expression Connie herself would have used—*napping? how lazy*—and the housekeeper's face shifted with agreement.

"She really should be awake by now," she said. "Why don't you go on up and tap? Last door on the left."

"Thanks." I moved past her, into what seemed a particularly female kind of quiet, probably because of all the pastel fabrics and delicate furniture. Up the stairs and down the hall to her door, where I knocked softly.

"Noooo . . ." Emory groaned. "Go away, Mom. Thought you were at a flower show."

"It's Jamie Atkinson."

Silence. Rustling. Then the door cracked open. Had she been crying? The skin beneath her tear-bright eyes was pink, but her face was tight with suspicion.

"Jamie. Nobody sent you here, did they?"

"Me? No."

"Like Sebastian? To cheer me up? Because I don't want any cheering up right now."

"I promise, I wasn't sent. But I can come back another time, if you want."

Whatever flimsy excuse I'd planned for why I'd dropped in on her, Emory didn't seem to need a reason. In fact, it struck me, as she opened the door wider for me to step through, that maybe she'd been hoping for company—anyone's, even mine. "My room's a pit these days," she semi-apologized, with a sniffle.

"Don't worry about it—mine always is." I stepped in. Her room looked like it had been decorated by a messy mermaid. Lots of shiny purple and white wicker, conch shells and open fans. I picked up a desk photo of her and Jessie, arms slung over each other's shoulders, both with tangled hair and smiles, caught in a moment of uncomplicated summertime radiance.

"Our last picture," said Emory. "For months, it was too hard to look at. I only put it up again last week."

Suddenly I was tremendously envious of that picture. Its beachy innocence needled at me. When was the last time I'd felt so carefree? When had Mags and I last enjoyed a laugh? I'd been sulking and depressed all spring, without the nerve to tell her— I'd made up a hundred different reasons (the twins graduating, my back injury, my C in European history) to disguise the secret, shameful one—and we'd been apart most of this summer. Would things go back to normal with us come fall? I hated to think that they wouldn't.

I stuck the picture back on the desk, maybe too hard.

"Hey." She swept it up against her chest and stared at me, her eyes narrowed. "What's wrong with you?"

"Nothing. Sorry. Really."

"Why're you rubbing your back?"

"Oh. It's this old injury. I didn't think biking would make it worse. I was wrong, I guess."

Emory placed the photo faceup deep in the corner of her windowsill, as if to guard me from attacking it. But then, studying me, she seemed to relent. "I've got OxyContin."

"Yeah? I could use some."

She disappeared into her bathroom and returned with the pill and a glass of water.

"Why do you have OxyContin?" I asked. "What's wrong with *you?*"

"Left over from my wisdom teeth. But I just took one twenty minutes ago. Wisdom teeth are a joke, compared with this."

152

"With what?"

"Aidan broke up with me. I thought everyone knew. I *know* Sebastian knows." Emory shook back her hair, her cool-girl confidence hanging by a thread as she dropped back into her bed and buried most of herself in the duvet. "Sunrise Dry Cleaners is like the gossip nucleus of Bly."

"He came by for a swim yesterday, and he didn't tell me anything," I answered honestly. "But he was only around for a little while to cool off." Sebastian's after-work visits, though they ended all too soon, were the highlight of my day. And he never gossiped. He'd spent most of yesterday's visit helping Isa perfect her half gainer. "What happened?"

"You'll have to ask Aidan. He says it's for every reason in the world except Lizbeth Paley. But then why would he do it on the phone? Before the weekend? I'll tell you why—because he wants to be single this weekend," she answered her own question with a short, unhappy laugh. "Because guess who just broke up with her high school boyfriend?"

She did seem to want an answer. "Lizbeth Paley," I ventured.

"Exactamundo." She nodded toward the pill in my hand. "You better go for it. It's gonna melt." As I downed it, Emory watched, leaning back over her purple satin mermaid pillows, while I stayed perched upright like a sea horse at the end of her bed.

"I never liked Aidan," I said, braving it. "He was always coming on to me, if you want to know the truth. And only because I look like Jessie. He was way too fascinated by the similarity; he made it uncomfortable for me every time."

Emory flicked her fingers. "Those aren't Pentagon secrets. Everyone knew about Aidan's being hot for Jessie."

"Oh." I faltered. "But you and Aidan stayed together anyway."

"Sort of. He goes to boarding school up in New Hampshire, I'm in Boston—maybe the distance made us closer. Especially when you just want someone to talk to late at night. By the time we saw each other this summer, it was like we just fell back in the habit of dating." Emory had the apologetic-defiance thing down cold. I felt like she was ready to jump me with an answer no matter what question I asked.

"And you were still able to be friends with Jessie?"

Except that one. Emory seemed to droop a little. "With Jessie, it was more complicated. She was such a free spirit. It's like getting mad at the wind for blowing down your sand castle. And she loved Pete most of all—he was her soul mate. She liked to have fun, but Aidan was just a diversion. He wasn't anything to her."

"So, since it wasn't serious, that made it easier?"

"What can I say? Love makes you stupid."

"True." And while I couldn't tell if Emory was referring to Aidan or Jessie, it didn't seem too important to get her to clarify. *Love makes you stupid.* Yeah, I got that.

Emory's wooziness level had seemed to up a notch as she now regarded me. "Not that you need to worry. Sebastian Brooks is hot and smart, with the added benefit that he's actually a decent guy," she said. "You could do way worse. He was off the market all last year. Fact is, none of the Little Bly couples from last year have stayed together. Well, except for Peter and Jess. I'm not sure that they count, though."

"I'd heard Peter and Jessie had problems, those last days." I went slow, feeling my way through this new opportunity window. This was, after all, why I'd come out here. To find out more. To learn the truth, or as close to the truth as Jessie's best friend might know. "That they'd been fighting."

"Really? Where'd you hear that, from Mother Hubbard? 'Cause that's news to me." Emory frowned skeptically. "According to Isa, they were planning to get married that weekend."

It was like a brick drop straight to the foot. "Come on. That sounds like a joke."

"Who knows? Jessie'd never clued me in, and she was pretty impulsive. Anyway, it's the story Isa liked to tell, and she was so wrecked those first weeks after, we all figured she needed to believe in something nice—a happy ending in heaven." Emory yawned. She was turning boneless. She stretched her hands languorously over her head and slipped deeper under the covers. "It's not that incredible, if you knew Jess. She didn't want to go to college, she hated academic stuff. Last summer, she told me she never wanted to leave Bly. Didn't want to deal with senior year, period." Emory's bleary eyes suddenly met mine. "Oh my God. I'd never thought of it like this before, but Jess got her wish, right? In an ironic, tragic sort of way."

"Married . . ." I unfolded the word, which felt opaque, like a heavy, itchy lace. I couldn't believe it.

"That's why they were taking the Cessna to North Carolina. They'd planned to fly into Raleigh and drive to Georgia. You can get a marriage license in Georgia without your parents' permission. Or that's what Isa said Peter had told her. Eloping is always like one of those dare-ya's that kids talk about."

Married. No, that didn't make sense. Not according to Jessie's last note, or anything that Isa had ever said to me. "Did Peter ever really want to? I mean, for the . . . right reasons?" I asked.

"You mean, did he just want to marry her money?" Emory yawned. "Maybe. Pete always acted like money meant nothing to him, but what a joke, we all knew better. And he sure didn't say

155

no when Jess picked up his tabs at Green Hill. He used to dress in Mr. McRae's clothes. Watches, belts, blazers, all of it. And he sped around in McRae's Porsche so much it seemed like his."

"Was it obnoxious?"

"It could be grating. Pete loved to lord it over people. I'll never forget his face when he told me about Aidan and Jess. The triumph in it."

I cringed. "That sounds pretty low."

"Oh, that kid could be the king of low. The quickest path to making himself feel superior was to make other people feel bad." But Emory's speech had slowed to a crawl, and her eyes had given up trying to stay open. Ha, those were the days, when one OxyContin could do that to me.

"Jessie didn't care what other people thought. And Peter cared too much," I said.

Emory nodded. "Yrmm . . . 'Swut brought them together, I guess."

More than that, I thought. It was what had destroyed them.

TWENTY

The ringing wouldn't stop.

It had begun on the bike ride home. Droning yet quiet, a fly hovering outside swatting range. Not quite enough to be a full-on menace, but bothersome just the same. I went right downstairs, joining Isa for some TV to filter out the sound, then fell asleep watching a ballroom-dance marathon. Rousing only after Connie stomped down and shook me awake.

Later that night after dinner, as Isa and I played one of her favorite games she'd taught me, called M.A.S.H. (Mansion-Apartment-Shack-House), the sound had accelerated from fly to worse. And while I knew that nobody else could hear it, that it was all mine, somehow it sounded as if the noise were filtering in from elsewhere; through the water pipes, the radiator vents, the chimney flue. While it was subtle as a squirrel chewing through paneled wood for a way out *she shall have music wherever she goes,* its persistence was killing me.

I screwed my pinkies deep into my ears. Isa was talking to me.

"Come on, Jamie!" With a snap in my face. "You're not listening. Write it down: Veterinarian! Actress! Photographer! Doctor!"

"Okay, okay." I recorded her wish list of professions on the lined notebook paper.

"And what's wrong with your ears?"

"They're just buzzy. Maybe from swimming. What about your husband's profession?"

Isa got most of her top choices—in her M.A.S.H. life, she'd go on to enjoy a future as a Lamborghini-driving doctor with two kids and an acrobat husband, but she'd be living in a shack. "Oh, no! The shack ruins the whole life!" Her eyes blinked with outrage. "No matter how good everything else turns out, if I'm in that stinky shack, then everyone is laughing at me."

"Maybe you and your husband are living off the grid. You know, making an anti-consumer statement."

"Whatever. Name a single normal person who lives in a shack."

"You could always sell your Lamborghini and upgrade to a house."

"No." Isa shook her head with great conviction. "That's not what M.A.S.H. is. It's about your final destiny."

"M.A.S.H. is just a silly game." I flipped the paper. "Do you want to do mine?"

"The shack wrecked my mood. Let's go get Milo. He might be downstairs watching movies."

"You go." I didn't want to. Lately, Isa hadn't been too inter-

ested in tagging after Milo, or trying to include him in her enter-
tainments, which was a relief. Milo existed in a neutral background
these days—in other words, right where I wanted him.

After I'd settled Isa for the night, supplying her with a mug
of honey-sweetened milk and her nature DVDs, and I was in my
room getting ready for bed myself, I heard a scrape and thud
directly over my head. In moments, I was up on the third floor,
in the canopy bedroom. Where the curtains had been drawn—
who'd done that?—casting it in near total darkness. The only
light source was a blaze in the hearth, and Milo crouched in
front of it, prodding it with a fire iron.

"What's going on here? Did you open the flue?"

"Uh-huh." He didn't seem surprised or concerned to see me.
The fire's flames bathed him in a lurid orange half-light. "What's
it look like I'm doing? I'm burning stuff." He gave a few more
turns of the poker.

"What are you burning?" On a glance, just some papers.

"I write in a journal." He spoke below his breath, so that his
words weren't quite for me. "Because I like to see everything
written down. So that I know it really happened. That I wasn't
just making it up. Then I read it and memorize it. And then I
have to destroy the hard evidence."

I thought of my own journal, the muddle of every page. All
those unfiltered, lunatic letters to Sean Ryan.

"What is it, exactly, that you need to destroy?"

"Everything that I don't want to be true."

"Come downstairs."

"When the fire's dead, I will."

But I waited. It seemed irresponsible to leave Milo here,
unattended, while a fire was burning.

"We have more in common than you think, you and I," he said. The flickering light shadowed his face and shone reddish over his hair while siphoning the color from his eyes, and now he wasn't exactly Milo anymore. I blinked him back to form.

The ringing in my ears was erratic but at the same time quite painful: in one moment as loud as the clang of church bells and then morphing to a wet but staticky noise like a nature show's sound track amplified for some inaudible thing—the tunneling earthworm, the hatching larva. I fought a wave of fatigue as I leaned against the doorframe. "I wouldn't know about that," I told him. "Since I really don't know anything about you."

"But I know so many things about you." Was the smoke getting thicker? It was too dark to focus. The fire seemed to have raised the temperature of the room. And Milo's voice had deepened. Another trick, maybe.

"Like what?"

"You can see things that other people can't see." No, it was not Milo's voice. "Isn't that true? Because I'm always here, always. Even if the others can't sense me, you can, always."

"You brought me up to this room on purpose," I said faintly.

"We used to come here all the time," said Milo—though he wasn't Milo, not anymore. He had taken on the shape of Milo, he'd lured me upstairs and into this room as Milo, and now it was too late—he'd drawn me in. And I realized, a cold and sinking knowledge, that I couldn't consciously control what I saw anymore. Or what I heard.

"And we had a code, remember that?" he said. "She'd tell Isa to go to her room or the lighthouse or her playroom and—"

"You shouldn't have done that to Isa," I interrupted.

160

In profile he looked thoughtful but defiant. "No. Maybe not."

"You loved Jessie," I said. "And I do know how it feels to love someone who might not have returned that feeling with the same strength. Someone who maybe thought of you as a diversion, and who began to slip away from you before you were ready to let go. But love makes you stupid, and it was wrong—pointless and wrong—to hold on tighter to someone who was already gone. Gone from you, I mean."

He didn't answer. The room was warm, too warm. His skin seemed lit up by the fire—it threw off a radiance, sparks and heat. "And you're right," I continued, with as much assurance as I could muster, though I could hardly hear myself over the noise in my own ears. "You're always here, I sense you always, and there are times when I also see you very clearly, Peter. I wish I didn't. But you know that, don't you? You know how much I don't want to see you."

"It's nobody's choice, Jess," he said as he turned, and then all at once he'd closed the space between us in waves of heat and burning gasoline, smothering, a nearly unendurable furnace. But I didn't move to leave or stop him. It almost startled me how easily I closed my eyes, deadened my will, my limbs, and gave into accepting that—if only for the moment—it was all exactly as he said it was. Even as my logical mind struggled to assert that I was witnessing nothing more than persuasive magic of the darkness and my own troubled dream state, of course I knew that it was more.

TWENTY-ONE

How many minutes was I there? When did the fire go out, when did I break free from my vision to find myself alone with my terror? No idea, no idea. All I knew was that then I wrenched free, I became all motion, sprinting manic down the stairs, thudding the runner with my heels to feel the shock vibrate up my spine, humming a pop song to muffle the existing chaos in my ears. Reconnecting with my senses as if released from a spell. Straight to my room, where I locked my doors, locked my bedroom and then locked my bathroom—ridiculous gestures, really—and I showered in the harsh jet of cold water that left a taste of ice and iron in my mouth.

In acknowledging Peter Quint, I'd let him in. He'd used Milo to communicate because he'd sensed an impressionable contact in me. Same as Uncle Jim and Hank. I knew this in capital letters.

But now what? Did that mean he would follow me everywhere, always? Did I have to add his restless soul to the burdens I already carried?

I needed to medicate—badly—but I was down to my last handful, a little more than a dozen. Some painkillers, possibly another sleeping pill, some of Mom's button-cute muscle relaxers and four wimpy blue antihistamines. I popped a couple of the antihistamines anyway, to take the edge off, but they weren't much help.

Sleepless, I flipped and kicked for hours, and in the sleep-hushed hour before dawn, I finally crept downstairs for a bowl of cereal. Exhaustion unsteadied me, but it was still too dark to go outside, to run or bike or do anything to get out of my head.

Instead, I stole into the den and switched on the computer, fishing up Peter's Facebook, staring again at his wall and his photos, rereading his mail and looking for another way in. If I could unlock the secret of Peter, maybe then I'd have the key that might release us both from our obsession.

Pendleton. I'd searched for it before. Lots of things were called Pendleton. A men's discount clothing store in Warwick, Rhode Island. A breeder of King Charles spaniels in Los Angeles. But. The thought sparked. Peter Quint's Pendleton would likely be in Massachusetts.

My fingers raced to specify PENDLETON, MA, and soon I'd hit a home page of sunny skies and gentle faces and testimonials that promised a healthful stay at the Pendleton Mental Health Facility. Was this his Pendleton? Was it worth checking out? It wasn't a bad wager, and it was only thirty miles away, once I got off the ferry.

Peter had visited someplace called Pendleton one day before the crash. Had he been there to see someone specific? His mother fit this category—the *She* who was near but not visible, alive but not active in Peter's life. Or that's what Sebastian had said.

Morning light was creeping through the cracks. As day transformed the sky, I stole back upstairs and fell into bed. My bones were granite—if my bed had been an ocean, I'd have dropped straight to the bottom. Connie would be exasperated if I woke up too late. This was my last thought before sleep rescued me.

When I came to, noon was high and hot, and I was thinly bathed in sweat, the sheet sticking to my body, and when I got up, my hair lay damp on my neck and cheeks. Outside my bathroom window, I spied Isa in her bathing suit, lolling on a deck chair by the pool. She'd even brought out a pitcher plus two glasses of lemonade. As I watched, there was a rippling in the water, and then I saw Sebastian pull himself up to land, swipe a towel off the back of a chair, dry off, then flop down on his stomach on the chair next to Isa.

Sebastian to the rescue. I couldn't have wished for better.

"'She walks in beauty, like the night,'" he said, rolling over, his amber eyes bright with welcome when I came down in my bikini and cutoffs to join them a few minutes later. "That's what I was planning to quote if you slept all day long."

"Are you off today? You usually come over after work. I didn't expect you."

"Yeah, it's usually the result of someone dropping by unexpectedly. I'm doing deliveries today, but it got so hot I decided I had to jump in a pool before noon. But dang, *I* should have been an au pair this summer. I could definitely handle the diva hours."

In his tease, he'd deliberately put me on the hook. "I don't usually sleep in," I said, embarrassed. "Tell him, Isa."

"Hmmm," she said, "you do kinda, though, Jamie."

Sebastian unbuckled his watch. "There's an alarm built into it," he said. "And it's waterproof. You're all set. I'll take it back at the end of the summer." He strapped it to my wrist.

"Oh." The watch had heft, a cobalt face. I'd noticed and liked it before; it looked kind of manly fashionable. "Okay, then. Thanks." I touched my fingers to Sebastian's shoulder. He sprang to reaction as if he'd been waiting for it, folding his hand over mine, jumping up and using it as a lever to twist me against his body as he began moving us in locked, mechanical steps toward the pool's deep end.

"See, we'll test it. One hundred percent waterproof, promise."

"Noooo . . . !" But it was such a delicious thrill, the backs of my legs against the fronts of his legs. I was struggling and laughing, with Isa shyly chiming in as she watched us—until I gave up and Sebastian and I went smashing into the shock of water. By the time I'd pushed and sputtered to surface, he was in a crawl halfway down the length.

I caught up with him in the next lap, and for a few more we kept pace, sinking to turn identical flips against the wall, two, three, four . . . over and over until I stopped, my lungs burning, to hold the wall, exhausted. I'd really lost ground from my former athletic days. Swimming, that's what I should have been doing all along, the whole time I was here. I should have been keeping up with my physical-therapy exercises. Taking care of myself in these simple, sensible and obvious ways—why wasn't it ever a clear choice?

"Are you gonna pull down her top now?"

I blinked the water out of my eyes to see that Isa had come to the edge of the pool. Where she was inspecting us.

"Isa!" I heard my mother's voice in mine, all puritanical outrage.

"What? That's what Pete did with Jessie."

I was mortified, caught off guard, but Sebastian let out a playful growl as he reached one hand up out of the pool to clamp it around Isa's ankle. Then he pretended to bite it as he launched himself out of the pool, and the whole awkwardness of Isa's comment melted away into a game of tag.

"You're not a bad swimmer," he said to me later, after an exhausted Isa had trotted up to the house for a lemonade refill.

"I was into some sports—I ran track."

"Why'd you give it up?"

"It gave me up," I answered, a nonanswer. My coach had thought the injury shouldn't have stopped me from quitting the team. It seemed so far away, running track. The discipline, the energy, the urge to compete. Like I'd been this whole other person. "I threw out my back," I added quietly. "It's an old injury, but it still bothers me."

"They say swimming's good for that, right?" Sebastian readjusted the lounge chair so he was parallel to the sun, as he dropped on a pair of sunglasses. "I take pool over beach any day, probably on account of almost drowning in the ocean."

I stared. "When'd that happen?"

"Eh, long time ago, with my cousins. But if I ever need to access fear for drama class, I just tap into that day."

"Tap into it now, how about?"

Sebastian smiled, that flash of Movie Star Teeth, and my

stomach caved in appreciation. "We were all ten years old and horsing around. No big story there."

"C'mon, details. Were you in real danger? Did you ever have that moment where you thought . . . it was over?"

He looked at me curiously. "Details and danger, okay. So they held me in too long, and I lost consciousness. They figured I was playing dead, but when they let me up, there was water in my lungs and I wasn't breathing. Then Aunt Barb saved my life with chest compressions and mouth-to-mouth."

"Wow. Hooray for Aunt Barb."

"No joke. She still talks about it: she says I gave her a good fright."

"I bet." In my mind's eye, I saw him precisely. Flat on the sand, a skinny blue boy with dents beneath his eyes and the agitated hum of the crowd surrounding him, pressing in for a closer look.

"And yeah, to answer your question, I did think it was over. The way a kid thinks those kinda things, a little dislocated from it all—but those last seconds, my body giving up, I remember saying to myself, 'Bye, world. Hi, forever.'"

I closed my eyes. I'd thought that thought, too, in a different context. "It sounds like you were close."

He nodded. "Funny thing, I'm almost grateful it happened. Every time I jump in the water—even when I go back into ocean—I'm always incredibly humbled at how I got that second chance to live another day."

"What's so great about another day?"

Maybe it was my sharp tone. Sebastian checked me over. "Is that a rhetorical question?"

I smiled like it was, but I wanted to know. "More like an essay question."

He nodded in mock seriousness. "Ahem. For what it's worth, here's my essay: 'What's So Great about Another Day, by some dude named Sebastian Brooks.' Take today. Did you have any idea that the sky could really be this blue?" He pointed up.

"Thanks. Sometimes I forget where the sky is."

"Hide behind your sarcasm all you want, Miss Atkinson. But this color is like a whole new fresh coat of sky made just for us."

"Summer skies are always pretty," I said.

"Or how about Isa's lemonade? That's worth living for. Sweet and sour, with all that lemon pulp and mint like a salad at the bottom? Oh yeah, baby." He picked up a glass and shook it, then drained it.

"It's not bad," I concurred.

"Or what about that tiny chip in your front top tooth that I love to look at?"

I closed my mouth, my tongue searching for the chip. Its sandpaper edge. "I'm getting it filed next dentist's appointment," I told him.

"Don't. It's perfect. Just like the sky and the lemonade and this crystal-blue, arctic-cold pool water. So many things have conspired to make this day great. And it's not even lunchtime."

"Either you're the most optimistic person I've ever met in my life, or you're a truly accomplished actor."

Sebastian wriggled his eyebrows. "We'll have to hang out more, so you can decide." He snapped his T-shirt off the lounge chair and yanked it down over his head. "But now I gotta get moving. I'm doing deliveries today." Lacing his fingers through mine, he squeezed our hands into a single fist. "It's been brief, but real."

"I'm bummed about the brief part." And I was. I wished he could stay with me all day. Sebastian Brooks was the sanest thing in my life, probably.

Instead, I walked him out front, where the Sunrise Dry Cleaners minivan was parked. I whistled low.

"These are some pretty fierce wheels," he acknowledged. Then he quickly kissed me at the nape of my neck, catching me by surprise. My eyes moved to the kitchen, then to the upstairs window.

"Mrs. Hubbard is definitely spying," said Sebastian, reading my thoughts, his lips warm and pressed against my neck. "That's a crab apple old lady's duty. But it's not like we're up to anything taboo out here."

Which reminded me. "Did that sound strange to you, what Isa said, earlier? About Peter and Jessie?" I asked. "That whole pulling-down-the-top thing."

Sebastian slipped a few strands of my hair behind my ear. "Naw. Half of what Pete and Jess did, they did for show. And those kids weren't angels." Sebastian pulled his keys from his pocket and jingled them. He wasn't moving to climb inside the minivan, but he wasn't moving in for another kiss, either.

"Spill it," I told him. "What do you want to tell me?"

"Okay, listen, Jamie—I don't think you should let Isa's world dominate so big. Before you came down, she and I were hanging out poolside for a while, and I'm all for dramatic improv, but her imagination can spin her out pretty far."

"Sure," I agreed out loud, though I didn't agree, not at all.

"I don't want to get you defensive." He opened the van door and slid inside, lowering the music so that we could keep talking.

"Everyone's protective of Isa. We've all known her since she was a baby. So when I see her playing those games, I can't help feeling like you need to reel her in a little."

"She's got strong memories of last summer," I said. "Nightmares that she doesn't want to talk about. Jessie's presence was complicated, and Jessie's absence is still complicated. So no, I don't agree with you. Because I prefer to let Isa be a kid, if that's what makes her feel safe."

His eyes seemed to gauge me. "Jess and Pete weren't what I'd call an impeccable influence. But you're different, Jamie. You understand that little girl's world. That's why I feel like you could do more than just accept that she's lost inside it. Isa needs to outgrow being that same child Jessie took care of. She needs to step out of her past."

Sebastian wanted me to agree with him so much that I tried to meet him halfway. "I'll . . . think about that." And while I'd been considering telling him my agenda for today, now I mentally nixed that idea. No way would he approve.

Instead, we firmed up the plans for Finley Beach. Sebastian would pick me up at eight, we'd go to the concert, grab a bite to eat on the boardwalk and meet up with the whole gang at the Rickrack later.

"Looking forward to it," he said. "But be warned, I know all the lyrics to all their songs, and I'm not afraid to belt 'em out."

"You can't scare me."

"So don't go running to Aidan with your hands over your ears."

"Very funny."

A few more kisses—to hell with the Funsicle—and then the

minivan was rattling down the drive. And even after Sebastian was gone, his good spirits stayed with me. A night out listening to music with people my age, away from Skylark, with no Milo, no Isa, no Connie and definitely no pills to mess me up. If I could just hold on to the hope of this weekend, I could push through this next thing that I had to do.

TWENTY-TWO

"Isa," I called as I came back around the house to find that she'd returned to the pool with a fresh pitcher of lemonade, and now, glass in hand, was sunning herself on the lounge chair. "What're you up to today?"

She cocked her head. "Milo said he'd hang out with me when he gets home from golf."

I sat, swinging my legs over the edge of the pool. "Or—how about come with me off the island to visit someone?"

"Off Bly? Connie won't like that. Not at all." She stood, stretched and knelt by the pool to drag in the raft. Then she belly-flopped onto it, holding me captive waiting for her answer as she flipped over and used her foot to push off the side and spin herself in a languid circle. "She was always accusing Jessie of taking me off the island." Isa raised an eyebrow at me, letting me be the judge of what she wasn't admitting.

"Right. I was hoping we could keep this private." I looked up at the house. *Mrs. Hubbard is definitely spying,* Sebastian had said. And now that Sebastian was gone, this fact got under my skin. "So how about I'll just tell her we're going to Green Hill? Sound good?"

Isa considered this. "I'll wear my jean skirt that Connie says is too short, okay?"

"You drive a hard bargain. Deal."

"Deal." Isa had slipped her heart-shaped pink sunglasses back over her eyes, but I didn't need to peer into them to feel confident that she wouldn't sabotage me. And Connie could be relentless. Poking for specifics, and then she'd want me to do this favor and pick up that thing, and her lisping requests would be a nagging footnote to the trip.

Isa beat me into the house. She was dressed and ready in minutes.

No meds today, obviously. I couldn't drive the precious cargo of Isa with so much as a single antihistamine washing through my blood. Even though the muscles of my lower back cricked and my heart was beating so fast that at every mile marker, I had to actively resist the urge to wheel the car around and beat a full retreat.

I wasn't even sure I'd do it until the last minute, the final turnoff for the ferry.

"Weeee!" Isa shouted into the breeze.

"We," I agreed, less enthused.

It was expensive to transport the car on the ferry, so I'd brought all my money with me. Once we'd crossed, I used some of it to settle my doubts, taking Isa to a family-style restaurant with laminated menus and a juice glass of crayons on the table. Loading her up on chicken fingers and fries and hinting that maybe we'd make another stop at the Dairy Queen after Pendleton.

"Who're we visiting, again?" Isa asked as she used a fry to wipe up the bloody dregs from her ketchup puddle.

"A friend of my mom's, who's sick. She's staying in a kind of a nursing-home situation," I answered, working through my story out loud.

"An old lady?"

"I guess so."

"Some old ladies are sweet, but a lot of old ladies are mean and boring."

"It's a quick visit. Cross my heart."

"If she's the second category, I'll put my finger on my nose, which is code for don't make me talk to her."

"I'm not even sure she's there."

"Like this."

"I get the signal, Isa. Loud and clear."

We climbed back into the car. Isa slept, mouth wide open and peaceful—nice to see, considering all her fitful nights at Skylark. She didn't stir until we'd turned off at the exit and the outlying sweep of fields came into view.

There was nothing strange or scary about Pendleton. Nothing institutional or even like a British boarding school. But as soon as we pulled in through the harp-shaped gates and I began to follow the signs to parking, Isa snapped awake as if something had stuck her. "Oh no." She began to shake her head.

"Oh no, what?" My heart skipped a beat.

"Oh no, we're not stopping here, are we?" Worriedly, she jerked around her seat. "This is the loony bin."

"I don't think so. It's more of a health facility."

"You're wrong—it's where the crazies live. I don't get it. Pete's mom is your mom's friend?"

Here it was. First confirmation that a Katherine Quint was in residence here. I just hadn't figured on it coming from Isa. I attempted to sound relaxed. "So I take it you've been to Pendleton before?"

"A couple of times, with Pete and Jess. But, Jamie, you don't want to go anywhere near here. You really don't." Isa's hand was clenched around the door handle.

"Please, Isa? It's just for a few minutes."

"You lied, didn't you? Pete's mom isn't friends with your mom. She's a loony. She's not friends with anybody. Why do you want to see her, Jamie? Why, really?"

"Because she has something I need. Isa, stop looking at me like that. Give me twenty minutes, and then I'll do anything— I'll buy you two Blizzards from Dairy Queen, both your picks, and you can give me the one you don't like as much."

"Ten minutes," said Isa, wary but resigned.

We parked around back and got out of the car. Isa glared at the building. "Connie would be mad if she knew you were taking me here. She got really angry at Jessie about it. It makes my stomach hurt, doing all these same things with you that I did with her."

"I'm sorry, Isa. Like I said, we'll be quick." Though my own mind was a whirligig as we began to walk toward the glass lobby doors. "You're very chill to put up with me." But I felt terrible, even as I had to ask her, "And would you please, please, please not tell Connie about this trip?"

"You better hope I don't. Connie says this is no place to bring

175

a young person." But then on impulse she clutched my hand, an assuring squeeze and drop. "Okay," she said softly. "I won't tell." Then her voice lowered to a whisper. "Don't let her talk to me. She's a witch, Jamie. That's why she's locked up here. You can see how wrong she is just by her eyes, how they twitch all around."

"You don't even have to look at her, and I definitely won't ask you to talk to her." My mind reeled. But I couldn't stop now, I was so close, I had to keep chasing it. Whatever her mental state, Katherine Quint had seen Peter right at the end. She had to have noticed something, witnessed something.

In the main entrance of rubbery palms, its floor-through carpet vast and beige as a desert, I stopped at a security desk, where I showed my driver's license and got directions that landed us two floors up, at a half-moon-shaped nurses' station.

"I'm here to see Katherine Quint," I said to a nurse whose face was dominated by an intense pair of black-framed glasses. "I'm a family friend."

She entered the name and shook her head, displeased. "You're not on my log."

I steeled her in my eye, giving her my best Jessie. "I've visited a couple of times before, last year," I pressed. "Or maybe you recognize her?" As I pointed out Isa, who was aimlessly jiggling the knob of a vending machine down by the elevators.

The nurse looked from me to Isa and back again. Her stare softened. "You do look familiar. So does that pretty little girl. What are your names?"

"Isa McRae." I went for it. "And Jessie Feathering."

She nodded. "Yes, that's right. Good to see you again. One minute." She pulled on her cardigan and left her station, crossing to use a red wall phone on the other side of the room. It seemed like a lifetime of waiting until she nodded.

"Go on up," she said. "Katherine says she knows you both. You'll meet in the common room. Once I buzz you through, it's down the hall to the second sign-in desk."

We walked through. Isa dragging, me terrified but brisk.

Although I'd never seen her before, I recognized Katherine Quint immediately. She had Pete's broadly sloped shoulders and pale eyes, only hers were watery and watched me from under half-mast, crepe-y lids. Motionless in her armchair, one of the few stray pieces of furniture in the bare-bones recreation room, empty save one old man dozing in his wheelchair by the window, she did not appear at all surprised to see me. Cautiously, I came to stand a few feet away from her, nearer to the ladder-back chair that she did not invite me to sit in.

Isa held back.

"You brought the girl," she said. Her voice was reedy and childish; it didn't seem to have aged along with the rest of her. "That wasn't your best idea, *Jessie*. She's a very susceptible child. High-strung, I remember, when the three of them came to visit."

"I had to take her. I'm her babysitter. I couldn't just leave her. And she helped me—she was a way in."

"Now all you'll need to do is figure a way to get out." The way Katherine said this was excessively hammy and theatrical, like a character in one of those early Hitchcock movies from the 1940s. If she meant it to be amusing, it only emphasized that she seemed off-key and off-kilter, a person sealed from modern technologies and preoccupations.

But I smiled, tight-lipped, anyway. It was not as if she could help living here. We studied each other, trying to make sense of the other's presence *round and round the cobbler's bench a monkey chased a weasel the monkey thought t'was all in fun*

"Hi, Mrs. Quint," said Isa, approaching to halt briefly at my side, just long enough to make a performance of touching her nose before she veered off to sort through a pile of old magazines strewn over a coffee table.

"So she's your ward now," said Katherine. "But you're not from the island, are you?"

"No, my name's Jamie Atkinson. I'm not from around here, but I'm living at Skylark this summer. I have Jessie's job, taking care of Isa."

Katherine Quint nodded, a tug of her head. Nothing in her face seemed to care anything about who I was or why I'd come here. "Then you were a summer friend of Peter's?" Her eyes twitched and blinked, reminding me of an old movie strip, and I understood what Isa had meant, that Katherine's "wrongness" was immediately apparent just from looking at her, from being seen by her. "He never mentioned you."

"This is my first summer on Little Bly. I never met him. Or Jessie. I've really got nothing to do with Bly."

"Nothing and everything." She sniffed but she'd grown rigid, and as her fingers began to twist up a tatty blanket across her lap, I sensed that my presence disturbed her. "And if you didn't know my son, then why are you standing in front of me?"

"Because he sent me," I said, with such calm it was as if I'd planned to say it all along to give her a fright or something, though I hadn't, not at all, and my own words hit me with the same atomic force that I saw in Katherine Quint's reaction.

178

It pulled down her guard. She straightened herself upright, but then just as quickly crumpled back in the chair, as if she'd lost her strength. But her energy had changed. Her eyes blinked around the room *the crazy people can always see clear down to the ugliest truth. Problem is, nobody believes 'em.*

"Who are you to me?" she asked. "Why should I speak to you?"

"I'm nobody. I came here because I need . . ." *All you need's a little proof.* "I need to be released from this burden, this weight that Peter's presence has put on me."

She was shifting in her seat, unwilling, angry, but I sensed that she knew exactly what I was telling her.

"So I came to find you, to see if there was anything you knew about Pete's last visit. It's not something I wanted. This history, Peter and Jessie, everything that happened last summer—I inherited it, in a way. I didn't choose it."

"What's *choice* got to do with anything?" snapped Katherine, blinking, shifting, and then it was almost a full minute before she decided to speak to me again. In the intervening silence, I could hear Isa, across the room, flipping through magazines and probably listening in. "Last time I saw my boy, he came alone, in that fancy car." Katherine's voice had gone flat as she relayed this information. "Same one you drove in, like he was the prince of Bly. He came for the ring to give her. The one his father'd given me, and his father him. I couldn't. Not at the time. I just couldn't. A mother knows."

"Knows . . . ?"

"When her child isn't loved enough." Katherine's gaze had found her lap and finally settled there. "I didn't give it to him, and I suppose I regret that now. I told him things I wish I hadn't. It

179

was his mistake to make. It was his ring, no use for me anymore." Her hand, blanched and formless as a peeled potato, suddenly reached out and seized my wrist.

And then I saw the ring on her pinkie finger—the only finger it must have fit, probably. The band was as thin as Christmas tinsel, the diamond hardly bigger than the sightless pupil of one of the portrait children. And I guessed at what would happen even in the split second before it did, as Katherine tugged off the ring and then closed my fingers around it.

"Take it back to Bly," she said quietly. Her eyes were soupy, so feverish, I could hardly stand to look at her. "And bury it at his grave. You'll do that for me, won't you?"

"Yes," I told her, faintly.

"Promise me?"

"Promise."

"And then you never come back here, never again, not in that fancy car, not any other time in any other car. I could spit in your face for how you look like her." She was leering, her lips curled back and revealing grayish gums, as if to show me she might make good on her threat right then. "A mother shouldn't have to see that same girl twice."

I drew back, nodding; I couldn't really muster outrage or fear when all I sensed was her maternal grief, unanchored and void, another kind of madness.

"Hi, Kate. May I interrupt for a minute?"

The male voice was so close and unexpected that I jumped to a soldier's stand, the ring clamped in my fist, my fist in my pocket, my heartbeat the pound of the surf in my ears.

The doctor smiled. "No need for ceremony." His name tag

read FELIX CAREY, MD. He looked young to be a doctor, but he held himself with the confidence of someone used to a lifetime of good grades and prizes.

"You're late, Felix," said Katherine, all petulant and sugary girlish again. "Don't you know it's terrible to keep a woman waiting?"

A nurse brought over a handful of pills and a glass of water. A yellow oval, a blue capsule and two little white dots. My mouth went dry, wanting them. But Katherine's fingers grabbed so fast that a white pill fell to the carpet and had to be scrambled for.

"Oh dear," she murmured, and as she looked down, I saw that her hair was thinned in patches to a pinkish scalp. It made me queasy, like I'd caught a glimpse of her naked. She swallowed all her pills so greedily I had to look away.

"Felix, this is my niece," said Katherine. I could tell she enjoyed the tiny rebellion of this lie.

"A family visit." The doctor smiled agreeably. "And you are . . . ?"

"Just Jamie."

"Hello, Just Jamie." He smiled. How kind of you, his smile intimated, to spend time with your crazy aunt Katherine. If only he could see how I was shaking. Would he know me for what I really was? In a moment of digital clarity, I saw my whole life unfold as a game of chance. The acrobat or the veterinarian. The mansion or the shack. The committed or the dispossessed. The question was—did it depend on my will or my luck?

"Jamie?" The doctor was passing his hand over my face. "We lost you for a minute."

"I'm fine." I smiled. No, I wasn't lost. There was nothing

wrong with me. Dr. Felix Carey could sense that. He assumed I was on the winning team. Team Sane.

"She won't be coming back," said Katherine, singsong. "Hard as it is to leave. Once you're in, they always want you to stay awhile. But you know that already, don't you?" Her smile, wrung up too high in her face, was grotesque.

"Isa!" I wheeled around—I couldn't bear to be here another minute. "Isa, let's go!" Quick with my mumbled goodbyes, my excuses, grabbing for my bag and heading for the comfort of the red EXIT sign, my one hand sunk like a stone to the bottom of my pocket, the fingers of my other hand snapping for Isa, hurry hurry hurry *wee wee wee all the way home*.

TWENTY-THREE

"I saw," Isa whispered.

She hadn't said a thing, not one single thing the entire trip home. We'd skipped the Dairy Queen—she hadn't wanted it—and we'd hit some traffic delays before the ferry. Now it was half past seven, way late for dinner, and we both were tired.

But now I realized that Isa was more than just tired.

I looked over. Nobody was on Bush Road and so we were cruising it, the wind picking up Isa's long, dark hair in a snap and billow. I couldn't see her face. "Saw what?"

"Saw her give you the ring. The ring she wouldn't give him, that he wanted to give Jess."

"Isa." My heart was in a sudden skip-rope. "What do you know about that?"

"Everything."

I waited. It was a full minute before she continued.

"The day. The day . . . before. Peter came back to Skylark from visiting his mom. He was looking for Jessie. She'd biked to town to pick up some things. We were all going to Green Hill later. Connie was out back, in her garden. It was only Peter and me in the kitchen. And he was so mad."

My hands were shaking. I pulled the car off the road. I didn't trust myself to drive. I maneuvered us to a safe spot in the meadow and braked. The grasses here were long, higher than the car door, and the sky burned with the wild reds of sundown. Shifting in my seat, I looked at Isa, whose face was labored with memory, though she was working as hard as she could to contain herself.

"Go ahead, Isa. I'm listening."

"I don't know if I can say it. I never did before. Out loud, I mean."

My fingers touched her shoulder. "Another time, then. But it might make you feel better, to let it go."

"He was really angry at his mom," she blurted, "for saying Jess was spoiled and silly and not worth the family engagement ring."

"He told you that?"

She nodded. "He was slamming things around. He said it was *his* ring. His ring for Jessie. And that's when I told him what I'd seen."

"What, Isa? What had you seen?"

It couldn't have been more than five seconds, but time made no sense to me; the moment before her confession was nearly unendurable for us both. "Jessie and Aidan," she whispered. "I saw them from the lighthouse. She'd taken Aidan up to the third floor. All I meant to do was explain that maybe Jess didn't want that ring, either. Not yet, anyhow. But then, what he did . . . after I told him. What he did . . ."

"What?" I reached out and touched her shoulder. "What did he do, Isa?"

She had pulled herself into a ball, her arms belted around her knees, her toes locked at the edge of the seat. She spoke her memory as if still spellbound by it. "He was smiling. That scary smile, more like a mask. He got a long fireplace match from the kitchen drawer. He took the sugar bowl from the dining room. He called me into the dining room. I went in. It was too dark. He lit the match, he wanted . . . he wanted to melt the bowl. To ruin it. He was doing it right in front of me. The silver turned all blackish. He only burned around the bottom. Where you wouldn't be able to see it. I was scared."

I could imagine it perfectly. Pete's smile and the match like a jacklight, the firelight disfiguring his face, finding its hollows. "And then what?"

"He was laughing to himself. He said, 'Isa, here's a lesson you won't learn at school. When you believe something is perfect, don't be fooled. It just means you need to search harder for the defect. For what makes it worthless.'" Her hands covered her face. "Sometimes I hear him saying that in my dreams. Sometimes I wake up, and it's just like he'd been whispering it right in my ear."

"No, no. Those are just bad dreams." I shoved closer so that the weight of her body could fall against my support.

"It's all my fault."

"None of it's your fault, Isa. None of it."

185

"It is, though."

"Shh." As I smoothed her hair away from her face, she quieted.

"All Jess wanted him to know was that she wasn't ready," she whispered. "She was always saying she wasn't ready. That Pete was too clingy. She even told me she wouldn't be mad if I let it slip out that Aidan was hanging around. But then, when I did let it slip out, Pete . . . he ended up killing them both. He did, Jamie, didn't he?"

And even when I couldn't answer, she kept asking this question, as the sun dropped away and cast us in cooling shadows. *He did, didn't he, Jamie? Didn't he?*

TWENTY-FOUR

"You're taking me tonight, right? Per our deal?"

I whipped around, startled. "Don't you know how to knock?"

"Sorry." Milo didn't seem sorry at all as he ambled past me to sit in the armchair by my bookcase.

"And we don't have any deal, Milo." I reached for the Baggie on top of the bookshelf. I was really coming down to the last of my pills, and the one I'd taken an hour ago had been from Mom's muscle-relaxing stash. I knew from experience that its effects were next to nothing, maybe a pinch stronger than an ibuprofen. Which was comical, which was hardly any help at all.

Two days since Pendleton. I'd wanted to find out things, and now that I'd learned them, all I wanted to do was forget them. Peter had believed that we were fated to our destiny. That we had no choice, only the illusion of choice. Was that the thought he'd held on to when he brought down the plane?

I pushed it out of my mind. Refused to dwell there. Most of the time I'd spent comforting Isa, who had gone into a bit of a shock since her confession. Now I understood why she thought about it all the time, why it still frightened her. She had needed to believe in their true love and romantic elopement to take the tarnish off the secret of Jessie's disloyalty and Peter's torment. Which was the truth?

I'd also written Mom, but I hadn't sent that note yet. My saved draft was a safety blanket. I pulled it out and wrapped myself in it, imagining her and Dad coming out to Bly to collect me. But I couldn't go home, or make any decisions that stuck, not yet, and Isa was the reason. She needed me now more than ever. I was her everything—big sister, friend, parent. Letting go of her secret had taken a toll, and I had to get her through it.

So if she wanted to play, I played. If she got bored, I found us a new game. When she whispered her nightmares, I shooed them off and comforted her, promised they weren't real. We dealt cards and built worlds out of the Sims. We dozed through narratives of forests and oceans and penguins on Blu-ray. We picked mint and squeezed lemons for lemonade, we tossed and caught popcorn in our mouths and left Connie to vacuum the stray kernels.

Yesterday we went to Green Hill, where I'd hung out with Sebastian when he'd swung by to see me after work, and then the three of us caught a movie in town. I almost dropped the whole story on him right then. But Isa had been right there, and somewhere between the Mud Hut ice creams and the ride back, I'd lost my nerve.

But tonight I'd tell him. Not just about Jessie and Peter, but about Hank and Uncle Jim, about Pendleton and Katherine and

Isa's confession. Even if Sebastian thought that every single word I spoke was madness, he'd hear me out, and I needed his logic more than ever.

"You look spacey. Are you okay to drive?" Milo's question was written deeper in his eyes.

"I won't be driving. Sebastian's picking me up on his bike, so you can't come with us. We've got some private things to talk about."

"You should sober up and drive yourself anyway. You've known that guy for, like, three weeks? Last thing you need is him in control of transportation. And you promised, you *swore*, that you'd take me next time."

"Why is it that I always have to deal with you, Milo, right before I see Sebastian?"

"Maybe because you and I both know you haven't learned anything from your crushed little schoolgirl heart. And Bass is bored, like I keep telling you. He's using you till something better happens. Same as the other guy."

"When and what have I ever told you about another guy?"

At that, he winked. "Maybe you don't need to. Let me phrase it real simple. Do you always put out on the third date, Jersey Girl?"

"Shut *up*! I never—" And I sprang forward and cracked a slap across his face. Its bullwhip sound jarred me as much as it did Milo. Who jumped up, holding his cheek.

"Oh my God. I'm so sorry." More like horrified. Where was my sense? I was too jumpy, had been since Pendleton, and I needed to relax. I could almost feel the blaze of the slap across my own cheek. "I don't—I shouldn't have done that."

He'd backed off me. I knew he found me ridiculous, maybe even pitiful. "Try to hurt me all you want. My point stays the same—you don't want to make Sebastian think you're ready for easy action." And with that, Milo had done it again. He was the maestro of cutting me down to my tiniest, most insecure self. How could I enjoy the night if I thought Sebastian was working an advantage over me?

"Fine," I told him. "You win, Milo. Then again, you always win. I'll drive myself, and give you a ride into Finley, too, okay? I'll send Sebastian a message that I'll meet up with him later. Does that work?"

"Yeah." He nodded, vaguely relieved. "Yeah, that works. Thanks."

I texted Sebastian the change in plans, but of course Milo's comment was now stuck like gum to the back of my brain. Did Sebastian see me as some party girl? Not from a privileged Bly background, and therefore less high-maintenance, more "fun"?

If there was a sliver of chance that Milo was right—that Sebastian thought I was looking for some no-strings summer hookup—it would definitely be better to have my own car. But I really hoped it wasn't true. I needed a friend tonight, and I was extremely hopeful that I had one in Sebastian.

And on my way out, a new obstacle. Connie was waiting for me at the bottom of the stairs. She looked even more sourpuss than usual.

"Thanks again for watching Isa tonight," I said, by way of truce, though I hadn't thanked her a first time. "I'll be home by midnight, if not before." Her expression bridled me. "What? Is something wrong?"

"You took Itha to Pendleton. One of the doctorth there recognithed her and called Dr. Hugh."

I reddened. Busted. "It was such a beautiful day," I said. "Isa needed the change. She told me she wanted to go."

"Itha *wanted* to go? No, I don't think that'th the truth. In fact, I know very different. And another thing I know ith that, for whatever ungodly reathon, you"—and now Connie's finger crooked on me like a mini meat hook—"*you*, Jamie Atkinthon, are *obthethed* with Peter Quint, and you're dragging everyone down into thith thinkhole with you. You had no right to lie. You had no right to take Itha to Pendleton."

"I said I was sorry. And she was never, ever in danger."

"That'th not the point." Connie stepped nearer. Her face was so close that I could see liver spots like fungus on her flesh, and the one rogue nose hair that I wanted to reach out and tweeze. "I'd have never, ever taken that child off Bly without her father'th permithion." A tiny dot of her saliva landed on my cheek.

"Well, I'm not you, Connie."

"You think I'm blind. But I watch. And I will thay it now— there might very well be thomething wrong with you, Jamie. Deeply wrong. Becauth dethpite your attention to Itha, and your kindneth to her—I'll give you that—it'th clear beyond doubt that you are unfit to care properly for that child."

I grimaced as I stepped away. The accusation was low and unfair. So maybe Pendleton hadn't been my best judgment call, but my care for Isa was almost always impeccable.

Connie was jealous that Isa liked me so much better.

"Let's talk about this when I get back," I said. "I'm sorry you're upset that I drove Isa off the island. I don't think it's done

191

her any permanent damage. It was a pretty day, we had a nice lunch, and—"

"Enough!" Connie put her hands over her ears and actually stamped her foot. "You quit that talk! I've got a call out to the Mithter! I'm taking thtepth! You're not to go anywhere near Itha! Do you underthtand? Do you hear me? Do you?"

"Of course I hear—I'm not deaf!" But her sudden temper had thrown me, and I would have bet anything that Isa was listening from upstairs in her room. My body was shaking as I brushed past Connie to the kitchen and swiped the car keys off the hook.

"Frankly, I'm glad to be getting a break from you," I called out. "And I'll be notifying Miles McRae myself about this conversation. You think there *might* be something wrong with me, but I *know* there's something wrong with you."

It undercut my bold words that I was speaking to the closed door between the pantry and foyer, but I was glad not to have to look at Connie. Was she serious, demanding that I not go near Isa? As in, a restraining order? Because of one stupid trip? What a wildly inappropriate overreaction. And she had the nerve to say I'd lost my sense of judgment? What a joke.

She might be only bluffing about getting in touch with McRae. But I wasn't. It was still too early to phone Hong Kong, but he'd be hearing from me later tonight. I'd be crystal clear, and I wouldn't mince words. Isa's dad needed to know about the real monsters in this house.

My entire body was buzzing from the confrontation. I left through the kitchen, backed the car out of the garage and blasted the sound system as I waited for Milo out front.

Take that, Funsicle.

TWENTY-FIVE

Twilight was precarious. Nothing but blind spots. I squinted. The road seemed extra twisty tonight.

"Watch it!" Milo shouted, covering my hand with his and swerving the steering wheel so that we nearly gutter-bumped. "You're all over the place."

"Sorry," I muttered. "But it was your idea to put me behind the wheel, remember?"

He didn't answer, but he bolted from the car the minute I'd nosed it and then parked it cautiously among the caravan of vehicles lined up along the turnoff to the beach. I watched as he strode far ahead, ignoring my calls, and before long I'd lost complete sight of him in the thick of strolling families.

Humidity was curling up my hair and turning my skin clammy beneath my striped hoodie dress. Bad outfit choice. Heavy where it lay against my arms and back, but so short that too much of my legs were left exposed and defenseless against the cold ocean breeze.

My eyes hunted Sebastian. I was frantic to see him. Also, he hadn't answered my text. Probably meant nothing. Still. I walked to the boardwalk and bought a funnel cake. Then I took a seat at a beachside table, where I had a good view for watching the band set up their equipment and speakers as the sun went down.

I checked my voice mail, rechecked texts, and then my voice mail again. Nope.

Aidan and Lizbeth were standing out in the surf, talking with some kids I didn't know. Lizbeth's hair was coppery in the reflected tiki torches that spiked the dunes. A ways apart, Emory and Noogie had snapped out a quilt. Staking a four-cornered claim that was equidistant from boardwalk, ocean and stage.

I signaled and shouted to the girls, then plunged like a kite through the crowd. On sight of me, a look passed between them. A not-entirely-positive look. Beyond that, it was hard to interpret it.

But I slowed my steps anyway.

"Jamie, what's that mark on your cheek?" Emory touched her own. "Your blusher is totally uneven."

I pressed my hand to my face. "I'm not wearing any makeup," I said, though I was—but just a little. Not a Jersey Girl amount, not to draw attention.

"So where's, um, *Milo McRae?*" asked Noogie. Taffy-pulling his name. By now, she and Emory had sprawled out on the quilt. Hands propped, legs stretched, toes ballerina-pointed. I decided not to take a space next to them. I wasn't feeling nearly welcome enough.

"I don't know," I said honestly.

"Sebastian told me you and Milo came together." Emory arched her eyebrow.

"Oh, I . . ." I was confused. Why did she sound sarcastic? And why did they care where Milo was? I couldn't take it personally. I hardly knew her, after all. But I'd thought we'd had a little bit of an alliance.

And now Aidan and Lizbeth had joined up with them. I fully expected the Aidan factor to be awkward, but it was more civilized, with Lizbeth kicking off her flops and dropping to sit crosslegged on the quilt. Emory didn't seem perturbed. The bond between lifers certainly didn't extend to me. In fact, I was the odd one out. I felt self-conscious and embarrassed without knowing exactly why. My eyes scanned for Sebastian—where *was* he?

"I'll just go for those drinks," said Aidan. "Jamie, you want anything?" Though he hardly seemed to be listening as I told him no thanks, and he took off.

"So, I am super curious, Jamie," said Lizbeth, with a little condescending giggle. "We all are. Where in the world did Milo go?"

"He went to see his friends," I answered. "I mean, he's definitely *not* hanging around me tonight, if you're looking for him."

"Oh yes. He is very, very hard to find," said Lizbeth, nodding. "Didja hear that, Noogs?" She tapped her toe against Noogie's ankle. "Milo's with his friends. So now Jamie can relax. Unless she's the designated driver?" There it was again, that smirking condescension. "Or is *Milo* driving?"

"Milo's only fourteen," I said. "He's a kid. He can't drive. Not on my watch, anyhow."

"Oh, right. Milo's *fourteen*. I think Isa told me that once." Noogie barked a laugh and clapped her hands together. Her attitude toward me was an improvement over Lizbeth's, but I wouldn't have called it nice. "You're sure a stickler for the facts, Jamers."

I couldn't answer. I didn't like how this was going at all. The static had begun again in my ears, worse than ever. I pushed my fingers against them *little girl blue come blow your horn* as I stared at Noogie, uncomprehending. Had I pegged her wrong? Was she a complete fake, the kind of girl who took on whatever personality was most convenient for the moment she was in? I knew girls at school like that.

Or—worse thought—Noogie and Lizbeth believed that I was some stealthy cougar girl all hot for Milo? "Hey, look, there's nothing between Milo and me. If that's what you're insinuating," I blurted. "I mean, please. I'd never hook up with a fourteen-year-old." Did I sound like a liar? Did they know about Sean Ryan?

What *did* they know?

They were laughing now. Really laughing at me. What was all this attitude about? It was as if they'd all gotten together and decided I was

"Let it go, Jamers," said Noogie. She was using her lifeguard voice, the one that usually came with a shrill, reprimanding whistle.

"Let what go?" Decided I was some kind of joke, some kind of Jersey Girl who

"You know what. You've got poor Connie Hubbard half out of her mind, wondering what wackadoodle thing you'll think up next."

Connie, of course. I was so naïve—of course Connie was the one spreading the stories. She'd already told everyone about my kidnapping Isa off to Pendleton. Now they'd rallied against me. Everyone on the island thought I was careless and irresponsible. Maybe they even knew about the pills; maybe they knew about Sean Ryan. Connie could have read my journal—come to think of it, I hadn't seen it around in a while.

Or . . . or maybe Sean Ryan somehow had found out about my job here, and had contacted Miles McRae in Hong Kong, and told him that I wasn't competent to take care of his daughter.

My thoughts weren't lining up logically *the sheep's in the meadow the cow's in the corn where is the girl* and part of me knew that, but the ideas were shooting too fast through my head and unstoppable now, *round and round the cobbler's bench* and my ears were ringing and my body felt unable to support the pressure *she's under the haystack* of all the accusations.

Hold on to yourself she's under the haystack. I stared from Noogie to Lizbeth. "Stop laughing," I commanded them. I began to back away. *I'm under the haystack fast asleep.* "I mean it. Stop laughing at me."

Noogie stopped. "Jamie," she said. "It's only because we're . . . we can't help . . ." She reached out a hand as if I were standing on a ledge.

"Help what?" I demanded. "Help how?" In answer, they gaped; nobody was going to step forward, nobody wanted to tell me the big secret when they could all stand around laughing at me. I couldn't bear it and without another word, I turned away. Running for the sea *the haystack the haystack,* which suddenly looked so inviting, the rolling waves were beckoning me.

197

I waded out into the darkness. My ankles were sucked up in wet sand as the salt water lapped cold around my knees. I filled my lungs with deep breaths of salty air. My skin and hair turned sticky, my ears were corrosive with sound, but the promise of a calm on the horizon was so seductive *fast asleep I'm fast asleep* I'd just keep walking, yes, that's what I'd do, farther and farther until I couldn't

"Jamie?"

I whipped around. The klieg lights from the stage were lit up behind him, so Sebastian was all outline, like a paper cutout. I could have hugged him, but there was a formality in the way he held himself that stopped me. Oh no. Not Sebastian, too. Whatever they'd thought I'd done, I couldn't begin to deal with the idea that he'd joined them, and that everyone was against me tonight.

"Oh, hi! I'm so glad you're here," I said anyway, blinking back the sting in my eyes. "When you didn't text me back, I thought you were upset about Milo."

"Confused," he said after a pause. "I was more like confused."

It was a warning of sorts, but I was just so relieved to see him, I ignored it. "Something's going on, Sebastian. It's like everyone— Noogie, Emory, Aidan, Lizbeth, even Connie are all acting so incredibly strange. As if there's this big joke on me, and they won't tell me why."

His head tilted. He didn't answer.

"You know something about it, don't you? You have to tell me. Tell me!"

"Listen, Jamie. Mrs. Hubbard called my mom. She might have called other people, too. You know how it is around here.

And she thinks you're acting . . . not normal." He stepped forward, found my hand through the dark space and sealed his own over it, as if he'd figured out my desire to break for it.

"What a witch."

"Listen, she's not a bad old lady. She's worried. But Noogie and Lizbeth's laughing at you might be partly my fault. I was with some friends when your text came in. I told them about you coming with Milo, and kids thought it was a joke, so—" A deafening screech drowned him out. Some sound check guys had arrived onstage and were fiddling with the amplifiers.

"So what's the joke?" I shouted. "What am I not getting?" I was so confused.

"They're concerned about you, Jamie. We all are."

"About what?"

Now Sebastian began to walk into the surf, ankle-deep, then pushing forward as he cupped his hands and raised his voice to a shout above the racket, but I was still having trouble hearing him. "I . . . I tried to understand and . . . helping Isa and . . . gone way past the point of . . . anything for someone . . . you think . . . agrees with me . . . damaging."

I seized the word. "Damaging? Me, damaging?" It was outrageous. "What are you talking about? I've been a good—no, I've been a fantastic babysitter for Isa. Which that spoiled, selfish Jessie Feathering had no idea how to be. She used her job and that house as a place to hang out and party, to invite guys over—she'd lock Isa in her room sometimes, did you know that? She hardly cared about anyone but herself, and nobody called her out on it; you were all way too intimidated. Everyone here is so snobby, they can't even bring themselves to realize how self-centered she was—I'm not saying I'm perfect, but I've always got Isa in my heart, always and always." *and always and where is the girl who looks after the sheep she's under the haystack*

He'd stopped a few feet from me, and was shaking his head. "Jamie, you don't understand. That's not what this is about."

"Right, I get that now. It's not just money snobs, it's Bly snobs. It's like a law here. The don't-accept-the-outsider law. But I couldn't be the first person to realize Pete most likely brought down that plane. There's got to be some evidence. Nobody's saying that, though, are they? Even if it's true, even if he confessed it, nobody here would ever want to get involved with a scandal. Oh no, no. Not on Little Bly."

But Sebastian hadn't even let me finish, he'd been talking right back at me, his sentences bitten and spit. I could only hear him in phrases, even as I tried to listen though the chaos of my own emotions and all the noise around us, which seemed expressly generated to confuse and disorient me.

"—and that you set plates and cups . . . you talk to Milo, both of you, like he's right there, right in the room! Imagine . . . poor Mrs. Hubbard . . . you and Isa both pretending that Milo was a real person . . . every minute . . . all day. A game of . . . really screws up . . . lot of people, can't . . . get it? What's the matter with you, that you can't get that?"

He stopped. I stared at him, openmouthed. Then another speaker shorted as an electric-guitar chord whined and died. My ears vibrated; I had to cup my hands over them. Many more people had arrived on the beach, and were congregating, and the space was becoming claustrophobic.

"You're wrong, he's not dangerous!" I shouted. "He was a

brother for Isa. But he's more than that now, don't you see? He's how Peter opened the door."

Sebastian sliced his arm through the air as if to amputate my words. He was angry, but I pushed on, I had to. "Listen, please, it's true, I swear it. Peter's too close to me. What he did, it haunts him, and he knows I'm receptive, you can't feel him, not you with your perfect skies and your happy little—"

"Jamie, stop! Please! Stop!" Sebastian placed his hand up to my mouth without touching it. His other arm reached to grip my shoulder. "You need help—you really do, Jamie. And I want to help you."

"Help me? I can't even trust you, the way you're looking at me. Like I'm some kind of maniac." I wrenched away. "You people are all so suspicious, you've been watching me like a pack of weasels since the minute I came here. I don't know why I thought *you* were so different. You're just the same as all of them. Worse, even, because you tried so hard to trick me into liking you."

"Jamie!" he called, but I was running now, as fast as I could to get away from him, dodging through the crowd, looping the long way so he wouldn't catch me, then doubling back to where the car was parked.

They'd never believe me. None of them. Nobody would ever believe me. I'd always be alone. There was no point in explaining it. There was no point in sticking around.

TWENTY-SIX

The island had too many deer. You could see them rib-thin and mangy, wet warm eyes peering, frightened as Confederate soldiers searching for a route back home. I drove in the dark and I willed them *back, back* and I tried not to listen to the sounds in my ears, the sounds of static, of phones ringing for me *bring, brring* the sounds of dogs barking at me *rough, rough* the sounds that nobody else could hear.

Which way out of this noise?

I imagined myself, breathless as the moon, looking over this world but cradled safe in my dream of it. I imagined myself at peace from imagining, in the place where nothing needed to be compared or considered or valued. Crushed into the infinitesimal thing that I was before I was made to be me. I could get back there. Because I was not caught in the lights. I knew the path, even if I'd never felt so alone going down it.

At some point, I'd messed up the car—not sure how—and I'd punctured a tire. The hill was too steep to attempt with a flat. I wouldn't be able to manage it, and so I left the car at the bottom of the drive.

Got out and staggered uphill by foot the rest of the way.

The house loomed. I'd never hated it as much as tonight, and I ached with homesickness. I saw myself with the twins, shining flashlights from our backyard tent. There was Mom clapping her hands when I finally braved the slide at the playground. And Dad inventing the lyrics to a holiday carol as we added gumdrops to a kitchen-table gingerbread house.

Those days seemed very far away, and not entirely mine.

Isa was sleeping. Probably Connie, too. Milo was nowhere. I opened the door to his room. The same unused bedroom I'd discovered that first day.

The yellow room, Isa had called it. A nondescript guest room, neat as a pin and minus a guest, and yet Milo did live here, in his own way. He'd been real enough, a terrifyingly intimidating boy who spoke to all my own fears of what those Little Blyers were "really" like. Milo had made perfect sense to me. He'd been easy to control.

Until he had stopped being Milo.

I continued down the hall to my room, where I fell sideways across my bed. Shaking off my shoes, listening to them drop *plop*, *plop*.

How long did I sleep? An hour? I swallowed the last of my own pills and then tiptoed downstairs to Connie's bathroom. I could hear her coughing through the wall. I scooped handfuls of her drugstore meds and swallowed them dry.

In the study, I closed the door. In another version of tomorrow, there would be a scene. It was unavoidable. The phone call from Miles McRae. Followed by one from Mom and Dad. The indignant thpeeth from Connie. A quick decision, an online ticket, a silent drive to the ferry. I didn't care. I was so past caring and I didn't want tomorrow.

So I'd forged another tomorrow. And now I stretched out on the couch, dozing easily, and when I woke up, Peter was waiting for me in a haze and ripple of burning gasoline. I could feel the oil slick on his skin and soaking his clothes. I breathed myself inside his moment, when he'd crashed from one world into another.

Up close, Peter's pale eyes weren't particularly kind. But he hadn't been a particularly kind person. Nor frail and combustive like Hank, nor too frightened of this world, like Uncle Jim. Who were also here, in a sense, though it was only Peter's presence that counted tonight, as real and true as the moment he'd shifted into the negative, imagined space that had contained Milo.

But Milo had been a story and a secret. A fight in the mirror, a tussle with my insecurities, a scapegoat when I burned the pages of my journal, a reproving smack across my own cheek when my emotions threatened to destabilize me. Whereas Peter's soul was separate. And now he was here. Now, he had come for me.

I wanted to ask him things, and yet my questions seemed worthless, so I didn't. I stood and I followed him out of the study, through the front door and onto the porch. My feet were bare, but the sharp driveway pebbles didn't bother me, nor did the rough grass as we began to climb. I was gliding through a painless void, I'd leaped safely to an in-between place where nothing bothered me, not anymore.

Higher and farther. I knew where we were heading. I'd seen my destiny on my very first afternoon at Skylark. It hadn't been Jessie and Peter who'd jumped. It had been Peter and me.

The wind seemed to lift me from my toes—I felt as if I were floating. Peter's rhymes made a song in my head *Peter Peter pumpkin eater had a wife and couldn't keep her put her in a pumpkin shell and there he kept her very well* . . . A pumpkin shell, that didn't sound all bad . . . a shell was safe, a quiet place to crawl inside. I'd been looking for one myself.

"Isa," I murmured. Her falling nightmares had been warnings, and in the sound of my voice, I caught a rough snag of memory that woke me into the freezing gust of ocean spray stinging my face, the scream of nerves in my cut and bleeding feet, the animal fear beating in my chest as I saw that we'd come to a stand high on the outcropping of rock.

I closed my eyes.

A rejection of everything that is known, for an embrace of everything that isn't.

What a strange trade.

From far away, I thought I heard someone call my name.

TWENTY-SEVEN

I left Little Bly unconscious. Maybe that was the right way to go? Spirited from one underworld and into another. I'd once read that for some of us, all of life is a rehearsal for this instant. For others, it's pure impulse. No note, no warning. Only the moment.

The last thing I remember thinking, before I jumped, was that now I fully understood both paths.

When I came out of the coma, days later, I was first aware of my two fists, soft and empty, furled and stubborn, as my eyes opened on the green walls of Boston University Hospital, and I was reborn into a pain that screamed its massive appetite into every damaged cell of my body.

Days in, days lost. But eventually I surfaced, more or less, and I learned the nuts and bolts of what I had become. There was an implanted chest tube for my semi-collapsed lung. A steel rod in my femur where I'd fractured it in multiple places. A figure-eight splint around my shoulders to hold in place my snapped collarbone. One arm was encased in plaster and a sling. And as many dings and bruises as there was space on my body to show for them.

In other words, lucky to be alive.

"We're all going to get through this together, Jamie." At first, my mother's voice was my only universe. A familiar whorl of sound days before I could comprehend what she was saying, as I allowed her to creep slowly into my consciousness.

At some point, I also noticed that the ringing in my ears had stopped. It was one of the first questions I'd asked, and it had an answer: the noise had stopped because the medication—the *correct* medication, Dr. Shehadha stressed—was working.

"Auditory delusion is one in a network of controllable symptoms," she'd explained during one of those early-days rounds. "And it's easy to treat." She'd been so easy with the information, as if remarking on my left-handed serve or the chip in my tooth. Just another thing about me.

Shehadha, that was a pretty name, and something lifted in the recesses of my memory. Once I'd read a storybook about an Egyptian girl with that same last name, or similar.

"Egypt?" I hadn't even thought she'd heard me as I'd stared fuzzily at the letters on her name tag. It was an out-there question, borne on sedation. My thoracotomy tube had been removed earlier that morning, and my throat was a tunnel of sandpaper, my voice a croak of escape from it.

"You mean, as in the origin of my name?" She looked pleased. "Is that what you said, Egypt? You're right, it's Egyptian."

"What's wrong with me?"

The doctor's almond eyes sized me up. Mom's version of what had happened to me was heavy on tender loving care, but light on facts. But now Mom and Dad were downstairs in the cafeteria for lunch. I knew this because Mom had told me so about eleven times.

"We're going down for a bite to eat, honey. Do you understand, Jamie? Just a hop on over to the hospital cafeteria. To have lunch. We'll be back. Twenty minutes, tops."

After they'd left, I'd pressed the call button. I told the nurse I wanted Shehadha back. I needed to ask the kinds of questions that were harder to brave when parents were hanging around on the sidelines.

"I'm taking your curiosity as positive sign. We've been reducing the morphine. So you might be feeling less groggy." Dr. Shehadha had a broad, taut face like a fashion model, without a model's blank expression of having been recently beamed to earth. A face I could trust.

"I jumped," I said as the night came back to me in a cold brush.

Her expression neutralized. "You did."

"I remember," I told her, "but I can't remember why, exactly. It was like it happened to a different person."

"You were very disoriented and confused. Those are symptoms."

"Symptoms. Means. I have a . . ." My mind struggled to find the correct word. "Diagnosis?"

The doctor drew the room's one high stool closer to my hospital bed and sat, tucking her Crocs behind the bottom rung. Her narrow hands rested in her lap. Intimate, but serious.

"You ready?"

How should I know? I nodded.

"Okay. Here's the story, Jamie Susanna Atkinson. We scanned your brain-imaging patterns yesterday—do you remember that, after the EKG, when three people came from radiology and they had that machine with the big screen and the crane-type arm that swung around?"

I managed another nod.

Shehadha continued. "So. They took pictures of your heat-imaging patterns that measured your brain activity, and the results we got suggest a pattern that we associate with some type of psychosocial disease, such as schizophrenia, that, if detected in early stages, has a very successful—"

"Issat . . . a joke?" She'd delivered the word *schizophrenia* so quickly, blink and you missed it. I attempted to prop myself a little higher and immediately fell back into the unexpected explosion of pain. Every bone, every muscle.

She waited as I clicked away at the morphine button. Then: "Is landing in the emergency unit of this hospital due to two concurrent, near-successful suicide attempts your idea of a joke?"

"Two attempts?"

"Your blood was toxic."

I nodded. The empty Baggie, Connie's meds. "If it *is* a joke," I said, "then I'm not in on it."

"It's not your fault, Jamie," she said. "Not at all. You have a disease. The good news is that your disease is really, really treatable."

And then she introduced me to a few less-cheerful terms: *auditory delusion, hallucination, paranoia, somnambulism, catatonia,* and *depression.*

"In my family, we just call it mopey." Though even saying it, I felt like a traitor to my mom. Who seemed particularly wrecked. Especially when she and Dad returned from lunch to find out I'd learned everything.

"It's my fault, Jamie. I knew something wasn't . . . I just knew it."

"Mom, you didn't. You couldn't have."

"I should have." Her eyes were so sore-looking they made mine hurt.

Dad, carrier of the black marble, the Atkinson gene, could not seem to keep still for a minute. Then, and every other time he came to see me, all those long, lying-around days, he paced restless and uncertain. Always fiddling with the curtains and experimenting for the exactly correct fraction of shade to sunlight. Leaving Mom to talk about everything she'd done wrong in raising me.

A disease. It was hard to heal myself around that word, even as my bones fused and my bruises eased into softer color themes, though the scar up my thigh was a thick track of tissue, ugly as litter on the landscape of my skin. As much as I hated it, I knew that it would help me remember that there were many possible outcomes for what I'd done, and I was lucky that I'd escaped relatively unscathed.

I'd wanted to see Sebastian right from the first day, after I found out that he'd saved my life. My name in his voice had been the last sound I'd heard before I'd gone under. As I'd stood, paralyzed, he'd apparently called the coast guard and the police, and scrambled down and come in after me right after I'd jumped. Fighting against his own fears, dragging me to shore.

The first time Sebastian visited me, I wasn't ready. Too groggy, too battered, the tube still snaked in my throat, I'd muttered unintelligibly at him and assumed, as my puffy eyes watched him go, that this had been his courtesy visit and I'd never see him again. But that's what I'd always assumed with Sebastian, and I'd always been wrong.

The second time, after he called to check on me, and to tell me he was coming by, I was "ready." I'd gotten Mom to bring me my cosmetic kit—pitiable, really, the whole makeover attempt, combing my hair and fingertip-blending a concealor stick under my sea-monster eyes, while Sally, my attending nurse, watched with a face carefully null of reaction.

Those first visits, we talked about everything but the accident.

"Why do you keep coming back to me?" I croaked.

"You have this amazing energy, Jamie. For real," he said. "Maybe it's not always happy, but it's always right there."

"Sebastian, you're too much of a sucker for the drama."

"Well, and it's also the lip biting, and the chipped tooth," he said, bending to kiss my lips, puffed as they were. "You know I'll always be a sucker for that."

I continued to improve. My checkout day was established. Tess and Teddy returned from their respective pockets of the world, bringing me plushy Get Well animals and adventure stories. Mags came back with gossip and lectures and tears, sometimes all of it crammed into the same exhausting ten minutes.

And Sebastian. Always Sebastian, whenever he could. One afternoon he arrived with vast quantities of Rocco's takeout, carted in a brown paper bag and smelling like the sea. He climbed onto the narrow iron bed, and side by side, we spread out the feast. I finished my second fried clam sandwich before I picked up my nerve.

"Did you think there was something off with me all along?"

His side-view smile was heart-stoppingly sweet as he pretended to keep watching television. "Let me ask. Did *you* think there was something off with you?"

"Once I found a dead squirrel in the fireplace at Skylark," I told him. "He'd tried all winter to get out of that room. And I hate thinking about how he died; of starvation, probably, or exhaustion—but there must have been so much panic, before. You could see it, the way he'd chewed around the windows. That perfect, sealed view of the world. Sometimes I feel like that. Like I can't get to that other side, no matter how hard I try."

His silence was weighted as he mulled over it. "That sounds like something Pete said to me once."

"Did you ever think Pete brought down that plane on purpose?"

He shrugged. Eyes on the television again. "It's a rumor. There'll always be rumors about Pete. What he might have been capable of. They're both gone now. We've got to let them rest."

Of course there wasn't any hard truth or one explanation. If Sebastian had suspicions, he'd keep them to himself. He was still a local, a Bly boy, and he was too deeply attached to the island. Just like the Quints and Featherings and McNabbs and Hubbards and all the others, he'd guard his privacy. What did it matter? It had only mattered to me because of what Pete and I shared. And it still matters to me to have my truth. Every morning and evening, when Sally delivered my meds, I couldn't help but cast back to Katherine Quint, her cornered eyes and scrabbling fingers. I could do better than Katherine's life. I could do better than Pete's death. I could, and I would.

"You do realize this is my whole foreseeable future?" I asked Sebastian. Only half joking, and painfully aware that he knew it.

"Yeah, yeah. But I look at it this way—when I talk about my crazy girl back home, I can really back it up. Besides, I think a schiz girlfriend'll play well at Yale. Gives me some artistic cred."

"If I weren't bedridden, you'd get thwacked." I thwacked him with the pillow anyway. And then I made myself ask. "How's Isa?"

"She's dealing. If you want to look on the bright side of this whole thing—and I always big-time believe that there is one— her dad came home the day after your accident. Then the two of them went to Maryland to spend time with her grandmother."

"There you go, always finding that stupid bright side."

"Only because it's not hard to find."

"Do you think Isa hates me for disappointing her? For just abandoning her like I did?" Nothing, not one single thing, had struck me worse than this idea, and now I couldn't stop my tears. Sebastian pulled me in so that my head tucked neatly under his chin, and his arms were reassuringly tight. He promised she didn't hate me. He promised that she'd want me to call.

Sebastian left soon after. The next day, with a parent propping me up on either side and a physical therapy schedule, thick as a Bible, tucked under my arm, I checked out of the hospital and went home. Where, when I arrived back in my bedroom, the first thing I did was remove Katherine's ring, which I'd secreted in a side zip of my toiletries kit. Just seeing it again, the diamond winking like a sightless eye, set a chill through me as I slipped it into my jewelry box and, for the first time, turned its key.

Peter Quint's ring was not something I wanted to hold on to.

One day, I'd return to Little Bly, and I'd make good on my promise to Katherine. But that day was a long way off. Like everything else, I'd set out when I was ready, and not a minute before.

That same weekend, Sebastian took off for New Haven. Whenever he writes, I write back. I don't delete anything. I try not to second-guess myself. I let the hope for his letter in my inbox remind me that no matter what the weather is like, the sky really can be this blue.

October 20

Dear Jamie,

It's low season here at Little Bly, and Mr. M. and Isa are long gone home to Beacon Hill, and most of the other tourist types, too. So now it's just folks. I ran into Amanda Brooks the other day, and she told me you and her son, Sebastian, have kept up, and I was glad to hear. I'm not one to sit at a kitchen table with a writing tablet, but that's the situation I find myself in, so as to put down a few words to you. On account of how you'd left the island so abrupt, I believe there are a few things to make right.

Firstly, I am glad to hear from Amanda that you are healing. Secondly, Dr. Hugh has been by and he has set my understanding of your Condition. I will admit now that many's a time when I'd thought you were acting alarming and unruly—for example, how you would sleep till all hours, and burn paper on the third floor and generally put things in disarray. I am relieved to know it was not entirely due to your lack in Character. My Mother, before she passed, had bravely battled memory loss from Alzheimer's Disease, and Dr. Hugh assured me that your case is in some ways the same.

There's occasions I'm asked by others here— sometimes in an eager, gossipy tone I don't care for— to recount your visit to Skylark, and I have been questioned as to why I allowed you and Isa to indulge in your game of "Milo." To them, I say that I was pleased that Isa took to you so easy. Despite your failings in other areas, I can attest with Conviction that she blossomed under your care, and you must always keep Knowledge of that, when you look back on the less positive transpirings of this Summer.

My great-great-grandfather Winslow Hastings Horne was an esteemed Architect who was plagued by Visions and Sensitivities. He once said that those who suffer from watching the World the wrong way In can see Out too clear. Perhaps you can take Comfort in those words.

As for myself, I do feel it is my Duty, and perhaps the point of this letter, to note that I have come to a reluctant agreement with you, that the soul of Skylark is not at rest. And while I cannot put my sense of it to words, it is why I have decided to take my indefinite leave from the island. Over the years, I have put aside Savings, though as yet I have not seen very much of the world, nor any great Architecture beyond that of my famous kin. I plan to remedy that, and am looking forward to this next Adventure.

Regards,

Cornelia Hubbard

P.S. Please tell your parents I have released the Silhouette of W. H. Horne to the Southern New England Historical Society, where it may now be viewed by any of his curious Public.

ACKNOWLEDGMENTS

My heartfelt thanks to Charlotte Sheedy and Meredith Kaffel for being steadfast as ever and always. Also a big thank-you to Joan Rosen, whose insights never fail to brighten my in-box. I am grateful to Allison Wortche and to my editor, Joan Slattery, for the inestimable value of their time and thought as we measured and hammered and shifted and tested every moment of this story. Finally, I would be remiss not to mention my absolute debt to the Master, Henry James, for giving us the greatest ghost story ever written. Like so many before me, I have deeply enjoyed my turn.

ABOUT THE AUTHOR

Adele Griffin, a two-time National Book Award finalist (for *Where I Want to Be* and *Sons of Liberty*), is the acclaimed author of *The Julian Game*, *Picture the Dead*, the Vampire Island series, and many other books for young readers.

Adele lives with her husband and young daughter in Brooklyn, New York. Please visit her on the Web at adelegriffin.com.

Read an excerpt from

ALL YOU NEVER WANTED

by Adele Griffin

Available October 2012 from
Alfred A. Knopf Books for Young Readers

Excerpt from *All You Never Wanted*
Copyright © 2012 by Adele Griffin
Published in the United States by Alfred A. Knopf,
an imprint of Random House Children's Books,
a division of Random House, Inc., New York

She gets into the car and then she can't drive it. Can't even start the engine for the gift of the air conditioner. She is a living corpse roasting in sun-warmed leather. She can hear the quick death march of her heart. Her cell phone is slick in her hand; at any moment it might squeak from her grasp like a bar of soap. She needs to make one phone call, and she wishes she could make it into her past. Into last year. Or two years ago.

The houses are brick or stone fortresses guarded by holly and boxwood. Not to shut out the neighbors but to discourage them. It works. Alex realizes that she's never spoken with anyone from Round Hill Manor Estates. Not the people on either side of Camelot. Nor the people behind the hedges across the road.

In an emergency—short of screaming—she wouldn't know how to get hold of a single soul.

She feels like screaming now.

This story is nasty and everyone is spellbound and that's power. They're all hooked and I'm in focus, I'm mixing up this thing like I'm the smoothest bartender in the newest club for people who've all decided at this moment I'm one of them. And if there's guilt down my spine, it's nothing like the heat on my skin as I raise my voice to land it. Lies take nerve, which I'm working on. But nobody needs to know that.

"Don't quote me, but it took Gavin a week to cut the bubble gum out of his pubes." I paused. "Watermelon-flavored."

A moment. My breath held and a drum of blood in my ears. Oh, come on. Please believe it. It's way more fun to believe in it.

And then. Release. The table flooded over in laughter.

"Thea! Gross! That is so, so wrong!" The McBride twins were both buzzed on my words. Half-mast eyes while their minds writhed, thinking about who they should text or tell, and so what if my story wasn't one hundred percent or even ten percent true?

There are icky things people don't want to hear, like maybe if you peel some dead skin off the side of your toe and eat it. Nobody wants to know that. Then there's a Nasty that people love. And I'm good for that. I can bring that—even if it half scares me. There's a reward for the risk. Now all Emma—or was that her twin, Ali?—had to do was shift her chair so I could put down my tray.

The Figure Eight was made from two pushed-together round

tables in the cafeteria, where the McBrides sat at opposite ends like Cloned Queens of Disdain. And if it was too crowded, which it always was, you squeezed for exceptions, right? Except that with every ticking second, I could feel my alter ego, the girl I called Gia, curling up and smoking off into nothing as my real self touched down. Gia was my Topshop mannequin muse. Which sounds ridiculous, I know. A plastic muse. But there was something about her. Even when we'd stripped her naked or tarted her up in some cheap knockoff trend, Gia somehow held on to her value. She was made from style and indifference.

She was the girl I wanted to be. Could be, with practice.

The verdict on my bubble gum story would come from a McBride. Who both were studying me like we hadn't all grown up together. Hadn't done bus rides and field hockey and detention since middle school together.

Maybe they were remembering bookworm Thea. Maybe they'd forgotten that I'd already sat at the Figure Eight a handful of times this year.

Give it up, McBrides. Give me a seat and I'll invite you all to my house on Saturday night.

Give it to me and I'll never give it up.

Maybe they did know this. Maybe that was why they were hesitating?

"Theodora Parrott?"

I whipped around and almost bumped against Mr. Quigley, school secretary–slash–walking fossil, standing way too close. Had he overheard me? No way. Q was 186 years old and deaf as a worm. But my defenses zipped to attention. Whatever I'd done, I didn't need the blue slip.

"The front office wants you," wheezed Q. "Outside line. It's your sister."

At the mention of my sister, everyone got sober. And now my chance to sit was officially shot. All eyes were on me—everyone was looking for my worry. I shoved my lunch tray at Q's sternum. A little hard, for the joke. "Um, then, can you deal with this? Thanks."

"Oh!" As he jumped back, his knobbed fingers reflexively took the sides of the tray. I spun off, loose and free. Style and indifference. Thankful for the easy laughter in my wake, and hopeful that nobody would talk too much about Alex behind my back.

Insufferable. Last week, Mom called Alex that. For missing school, which is Al's new talent. Except *Insufferable* means nothing, since we all had to keep right on suffering Alex no matter what she did.

And now she wanted me to come home.

"Are you high?" I pressed a finger to my ear as I shifted the chunky black men's shoe of the school's phone receiver. Alex once told me that some phones at Greenwich Public—including the wooden phone box in the front hall—would never change because they were "quirky comfort objects." Preserved in amber, so that alums would be nostalgic and write checks at homecoming.

This quirky comfort object was complete with crackling static. "Alex, I can hardly hear you. I gotta go. I've got an orgo quiz next period."

"You don't get it. I'm stuck. I can't . . . I'm stuck."

"Call Joshua?"

"He's at work. His mom would combust with rage if he took off." Her voice was tin, a girl from outer space. Which she was, in a way. New Alex was a dried-up, lollipop-head alien of the big sister she used to be.

"Can't I leave after my quiz?"

"I wouldn't call unless I had to, Thee."

"Right." I'd lost. In fact, I'd already switched on my cell—an in-school no-no unless it was a 911—to text Mom in L.A. for official permission to leave school. But I wanted Alex to sweat.

She could suffer me a little.

Another five minutes, and I was backing out of the student parking lot.

My Beemer stuck out like a show pony among the Rabbits and Beetles and Wagons and Mini Coopers. I should have gone with basic black, not this hot villainess scarlet. It had been four months since I got the car on my sixteenth, but the car seemed the least-mine object of anything else in the pork barrel of Mom's remarriage. Less-mine than Camelot, less than my Gucci bag plopped like an overfed tabby cat on the seat beside me, less than my custard-blond highlights from the Marc DuBerry Salon. Maybe it's because I don't even really care about cars, outside of how much reaction I might jack from the fact that other people cared deeply about them.

Still, it was flashy. I should downtrade for a Jetta or something.

(Ouch, but that'd be hard. To that, from this.)

Another gilded day in Greenwich, Connecticut. Where even the birds sound like they get private singing lessons. Pulling through Round Hill Manor's security, then burning it around the winding drive, I dashed inside with a shout to Lulette in the kitchen. "Only Thea!"

And then straight upstairs and down the hall to Alex's room, knocking on her bedroom door. I was standing outside it when her text pinged.

in my car

Stuck in her car? Usually Alex was stuck in her room. Maybe stuck in motion was a good sign? Of improvement? I cracked the door to be sure. Uh-uh, no Alex. She must have seen me run into the house. I fled back downstairs and shortcut out the door. My footprints crushing an intruder's path all the way across the velvety green lawn.

Sliding into her Audi. She'd gone with navy. But you can't disguise that smug new-car smell. Same as mine.

"I'm here. What's up?"

Silence. A profile of pale skin and hollow bones. The short story: too thin. Alex might even be in worse shape since last week. She was for sure in worse shape since last month. So I hated the shard inside me—the Gia-shaped shard—that was thinking she'd better not kill my party plans for Saturday.

Mom and Arthur rarely went away when they didn't have Hector staying over to keep an eye on things. But this weekend Hector was taking off for his niece's wedding in the Adirondacks.

Which meant it was all going down right here. Party at the Parrotts'.

"Okay. Here I am," I said, a touch impatient. "I came when

you whistled. I blew off science. I ran a stop sign. Will you tell me what's wrong?"

But when Alex finally looked up, I was knocked speechless by how sad she appeared and how exquisitely beautiful her sad face was, and how complicated my feelings were about that. Alex has always been amazing-looking and never in a million years would I have thought it would come between us, and then I think maybe it did.

And I'm the worst kind of brat to admit that it was all over a guy.

But it was all over a guy.

Her guy.

There, out. See, when pressed, I can be exceptionally truthful.

Only I'd hardly had a chance to deal with that weirdness, because three months ago Alex went rogue, hyphy, off the rez. Whatever you want to call it, we all knew it had to do with *Haute*. Mom and I must have finished a hundred cups of tea between us, trying to crack *The Mystery of Haute*. Sometimes even poor old Arthur joined in, guilt pleating his forehead since he was the one who'd bought Alex the stupid fashion internship in the first place.

Alex wasn't talking. But whatever happened at that magazine this past January is at least semi-responsible for what's up now. Even I, with none of my big sister's looks and charm, even I can't wish whatever is happening to Alex on Alex.

"Don't you have to hit the slums for SKiP today?" "SKiP" stood for Senior Knowledge Project. Also known as something better for spring Greenwich Public High School seniors to do than cut class and go to the beach. By late May, most seniors hardly showed up at school. The rules got pretty lax. You could take off a week and still graduate. But Alex was hardwired to be more diligent than that. After dropping her internship at *Haute*, she'd switched her SKiP to Empty Hands—a tutoring center in the Bronx. One of the few things that still mattered to her.

"That was the plan." She sounded physically shot. Like she'd been attempting to get there by dogsled.

"There's time. I know you're worried about blowing off that kid you tutor, uh . . ."

"Leonard. He must hate me. Should hate me."

"He doesn't hate you. But don't focus on him right now. It only makes the pressure worse for you."

She nodded in half agreement. Dug in her bag and pulled out a stick of Orbit. I could feel her considering the gum, the way she second-guessed everything she ate and drank these days. Even gum. "That's like one of those sweet things you used to say, Thealonious."

She was kidding me; she meant in my geekstery days. Before I began the painstaking reinvention of Theodora Parrott. But Alex wouldn't have a clue how much effort Popular took. Alex never had to lift a finger to be adored. She'd have burst out laughing to learn how much I fretted and fumed to find the right anecdote for the Figure Eight. How hard I pushed to get myself to the best party on Saturday night.

"Let's just remember who's missing her organic chemistry quiz," I said, "that I now get the thrill of making up after school."

"I'm sorry." I could hear that she meant it. "But the thing is,

Thea, you're the only one who knows . . ." She stopped. I tried not to look desperate for the payoff end of that sentence.

What? What could I possibly know? What was so special about me? I wanted it so badly. But my sister's thoughts had gone traveling, touching off into distant places.

"Okay! Here's the plan! Last time you got stuck"—my voice was loud enough to jog her back to me—"you said the first five minutes are the worst. When you're overthinking it, you said."

"So?"

"So underthink it. Start the car and I'll drive with you five minutes. And then, if you can make it that far, let me out. I'll walk the mile or whatever back to the house."

"That's too far."

"It not. It's no problem. Really, Al."

Alex sagged forward. Rested her forehead on the steering wheel. Her dark, paper-smooth bob falling past her ears. "Look." Without moving the rest of her body, she raised her arm to show me the huge flapjack of sweat stain underneath.

"Are your wet pits supposed to scare me? Drive already."

"I need to relax. Tell me something. Take my mind off my mind."

My tale o' the bubble gum might do the trick. The germs of truth, and there are always germs, was that I really had seen Gavin and Gabby at Mim Goldsborough's party last Saturday. And Gabby really had been chewing watermelon-flavored gum in the kitchen. I'd caught the whiff. Then, when Gavin had blasted in with some friends, drunkly bungling through the cupboards for a snack, I'd seen Gabby's eyes fixate on him. Watched him brush-pivot-rub against her as he went for the bag of Pirate's Booty.

I hardly knew either of them. I'd barely spoken to Gabby Ferrell since sixth grade. Gavin Hayes, on the other hand, had always enjoyed his reputation.

The Nasty was like a pocketful of glitter in my closed fist. Too tempting not to toss in the air.

Days later, finessing the story, I swear, it was like it really had happened.

"So here's something funny," I began. "You know Gabby Ferrell? Well, the way I heard it, last weekend at Mim Goldsborough's, she got together with Gavin Hayes in the clothes closet of Mim's little brother's room. Big fat sloppy hookup. And the best part? The brother was sleeping six feet away."

"Making out inside a clothes closet. So what."

"Except it was a beej and they kept the door open. And—pause for effect—she didn't even take out her bubble gum. The way I heard it? She used her tongue to wrap the gum so that it—"

"Wait—did you say *Gavin Hayes?*" Alex fixed her fawn eyes on me. "But Gavin's been seeing that Russian girl for months."

"Oh, really?" My heart skittered. "He'd better hope this doesn't get out, then."

"With the big buckteeth but cute, the basketball player Coach Hal imported from Kiev so Greenwich had a shot to win State's. Everyone knows Gavin is really serious about her."

"Not according to my story."

"Your *story*. Cripes, Thea. 'The way I heard it.' You heard nothing. Voices in your head, maybe. That whole entire story's not true and you know it." As Alex dropped the unopened Orbit in her purse. Like I'd stolen her appetite for gum. "What is wrong with you?"

"Now hang on a second. How do you know it's not true? It could be true." I mean because seriously, it could be true, you know? Why not?

"Oh, get over yourself. I'm your sister, remember? The same sister who knows you've hated Gabby Ferrell since sixth grade when she made you cry at gymnastics, saying your feet smelled like a cat's ass."

"Hand to God, this story came to me straight from a McBride."

"You know what they call people who make up stuff like that? Mentally imbalanced."

"Wow. A lot of attitude from a girl who can't even get on the Merritt."

My comment refocused her. "At least I'm not *deliberately* sabotaging people."

"Look, forget about that story. You've got to drive. I mean, between you and me, if you don't try to make it to Empty Hands today, how do you expect to show up at UMass come September?"

"Thanks, Thea. Like I'm not far enough out on the edge here already."

"If I'm pushing you, it's for your own good. You're losing it, Alex." I was forcing myself to say it, knowing it was hard on us both. Truth can be physically painful. It sits so squeaky and worried in your chest. It releases so whispery thin. "This is insane. What if you're heading for shut-in? Nobody can read your mind. Nobody knows if your next act is to stop bathing and start talking to doll heads. So that by the time fall semester starts, you can't even cross state lines to—"

"Enough. I got it." She started the car and we jerked out onto the road.

I wasn't sure if she had it in her to drive. Getting a read on Alex lately was almost impossible. Like Mom said, you just had to suffer it. With full understanding that she was probably suffering it worse.